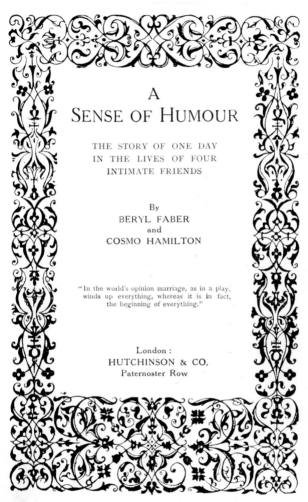

A
SENSE OF HUMOUR

THE STORY OF ONE DAY
IN THE LIVES OF FOUR
INTIMATE FRIENDS

By
BERYL FABER
and
COSMO HAMILTON

"In the world's opinion marriage, as in a play,
winds up everything, whereas it is in fact,
the beginning of everything."

London :
HUTCHINSON & CO.
Paternoster Row

UNIFORM WITH THIS VOLUME.

A SENSE OF HUMOUR

PART I

CHAPTER I

Hutton laughed, showing beneath his rather too obviously well-trained, well-cared-for moustache a set of small, strong, even teeth.

" Rather not, my dear Vi," he said. " Golf's a pretty good way of gettin' through the day, but give me my bed for at least nine hours. What ? "

Sir William Hutton laughed again, not because he thought that he had said anything amusing, but because he knew that he had confessed to his friend's wife that he was not so good a sportsman as his friend.

Mrs. Hay knew this, as she knew most things. For all that, she chuckled responsively, held her beautiful head on one side to show the exquisite line of her throat, looked steadily at her friend's husband without appearing to see him, and stretched out a bare, delicious arm for a small roll of butter.

Hutton gazed at Mrs. Hay with eyes in which he tried his hardest to put poetry, and when he asked if he might trouble her for another cup of coffee he said the commonplace words as though they were a quotation from Shakespeare's *Venus and Adonis*.

As Viola took his cup he manœuvred so that his hand might come in contact with hers—successfully.

"Only one lump of——"

Viola raised one pointed finger. "I possess a memory, Billy dear," she remarked.

"You're an emporium of everything that makes life worth the candle," said Hutton fervently.

This time it was the beautiful Mrs. Archibald Hay who laughed. And as she laughed—she laughed very well—she poured out the coffee with one hand and the milk with the other, easily, but with a pleasant touch of affectation.

"Dear me," she said, "if I didn't know your parents, I should say that you were a native of Cork. . . . And so, William, you have arrived at that time of life when you prefer bed to sport, eh ? Archie has been out practising mashie shots since daybreak."

" Good Lord, what a waste of time ! . . . Shall I give you a kidney ? " he added hurriedly.

Vi knew why he hurried. A little smile trembled round her lips. " Obviously," she said, " your memory is a very flabby thing. Now even after a fortnight spent under the same roof with you, I know that you hate tea for breakfast——"

" Wishy stuff ! "

" That you never indulge in more than one lump of sugar——"

" Why should I ? One's enough."

" Being, dear William, in a constant fear of encroaching fat——"

" Oh, that's rot," cried Hutton, wondering how on earth she had discovered a secret that he had not confided even to his wife. " We're a thin family."

Mrs. Hay sailed on. " That you must have a whisky-and-soda at eleven in order to look optimistically upon the world——"

" Why, of course. I'm not a beastly foreigner."

" And "—Mrs. Hay delivered her final indictment as though it were the ace of trumps—" that it is quite impossible for you to retire for the night without a mild cigar after a scorching bath."

Hutton was in the act of passing the toast-rack. His arm paused in mid-air, and his thick, reddish eyebrows rose high. " How the dickens do you know that ? " he asked with profound astonishment.

Before Mrs. Hay replied she picked up several crumbs and dropped them carefully into her plate.

" I have seen little mountains of your ash," she replied, "making a pattern on the bath-mat."

" By Jove, I'm sorry. Toast ? "

" I always eat bread, dear Billy."

Hutton dropped the toast-rack and pounced on a roll. " Yes, I know. I hadn't forgotten."

Mrs. Hay laughed again. It was the nearest thing to the song of a bird that Hutton had ever heard.

" What ingenious name do you call it by, then ? "

" No name. I only just didn't happen to remember, that's all."

And then they both laughed. Mrs. Hay

because she was amused at the man's bad logic, and Hutton because he was amused at her amusement, and her laughter was infectious.

He got up suddenly, crossed the hall, and lowered the blind over one of the diamond-paned windows through which a shaft of sun had found its way, and which having discovered Mrs. Hay, had been very content to nestle into her hair. Absurd as it may seem, there was something of jealousy in Hutton's action.

" Thank you," said Mrs. Hay.

On his way back, Hutton seized the opportunity of leaning over Mrs. Hay's chair. " You're . . . you're a delicious thing," he said softly.

Mrs. Hay raised her hand, barrier-wise. The expression in her eyes did not, however, convey any suggestion of barbed wire.

" I say, Vi," he added.

" Say away, Billy."

Hutton's voice took on a portentous and solemn note. " Do you honestly think that this idea of mine was wise ? "

" Which idea ? What do you mean ? "

" Why, the Missus and I sharing this golf cottage with you and Archie ? "

Viola went through all the usual routine of

thinking. " Wise," she echoed. " Wise ? . . . .
I don't quite follow the drift of your meaning."

" Oh yes you do," he said, catching up her
hand. " You know what I mean from A to Z.
I kissed you yesterday and now I want to go on
kissing you."

Mrs. Hay picked up a fork and held it like a
bayonet. " My dear Billy, *do* remember that
although we happen to be on the edge of a golf
course some miles from civilisation, we are
neither of us indigenous to the soil."

" Oh, dash long words, and do go easy with
that blessed fork. You're delicious. Let me
have another to keep me going."

" My dear Billy, please ! "

" Don't be silly. I'm only asking for one."

Gripping the hand that held the quite dangerous weapon, Hutton put his other arm round
Mrs. Hay's shoulder and bent down towards her
thrown-back head.

The door from the kitchen opened, and in the
twinkling of an eye Hutton was in his seat scoop-
ing out marmalade and Mrs. Hay was busy with
her coffee-cup.

Meakin entered, with a rack of hot toast.

CHAPTER II

MEAKIN had been Hutton's man since the year
that he came down from Oxford with his blue for
rowing, that is to say, for fourteen years. Born
a diplomatist, he never permitted an unquench-
able curiosity to merit reproof. He made the
entering of rooms at the wrong moment an art,
but when inside made stolid, respectful indifference another art.

Meakin was the son and the grandson of a
gentleman's gentleman. Both his father and his
grandfather had been with peers, and having
been pensioned off at the age of sixty, had invested their savings in keeping a house in Duke
Street, St. James's, with rooms for single gentlemen. The grandfather, James Meakin, who
had served Lord Alverton not only through all
his wild splendid days, but also when he suddenly
changed from a decorative to a useful member
of the community and developed into the level-
headed politician whose name will be handed
down to posterity as a determined opponent of
the Nonconformist smuggery and Little Eng-
landism of his day, made 22 Duke Street a very
much to be desired place, and was able to pick

and choose his tenants. He took noblemen, the sons and nephews of noblemen, the uncles and brothers of noblemen. He accepted diplomatists who were attached to the Embassies of respectable countries, and any Civil servant who had earned or jobbed a C.B. He also condescended to let to Army and Naval officers above the rank of captain, but on no consideration would he permit his rooms to be degraded by the presence of stockbrokers, financiers, artists, authors, or barristers. Once, in August, a well-known actor-manager dashed up in a hansom-cab, wearing the M.C.C. colours round his hat, and asked for a bedroom and a sitting-room for three weeks. He was rehearsing a new play to be produced early in September, and his magnificent house in Grosvenor Square was undergoing repairs. Thinking, possibly from the fact that he was clean-shaved, possibly because his voice was loud and ringing, that he was a distinguished Rear-Admiral, James Meakin saw him in his little sitting-room. Oh yes, he had two rooms, two very nice rooms, usually occupied by the Marquis of Buckinghamshire. What might be the would-be tenant's name?

As he had been the subject of a cartoon in

Vanity Fair and had hung in the glasses-only departments of hundreds of places of call for years, and, in addition, had been before the public as an actor for twenty years, the actor-manager was considerably surprised and not a little nettled to be asked who he was. He rapped out his name sharply, met instantly with a brusque " This way, if you please," and found himself standing on the doorstep gazing at a modest Early Victorian knocker.

Some years afterwards, when the public could no longer be persuaded to go and see him act, the actor-manager published two volumes of recollections, extremely ably dished up by a Fleet Street hack who had won the Newdigate. In it was told the story of how, when the actor-manager, whose love of practical joking was famous, called at a poky little lodging-house in Duke Street for rooms, he gave the name, on the spur of the moment, for the fun of the thing, of a distinguished Rear-Admiral and was hustled from the house. When, on ringing again, he handed in his card, he was, of course, received with obsequious delight and humble apologies by the old person, who had evidently been badly let in by the Rear-Admiral in question.

The son of this James Meakin followed in his

father's footsteps. He was an even more exemplary servant, who served one master faithfully for thirty-eight years, and who, out of a yearly wage of one hundred pounds, saved three hundred regularly. This Meakin also retired to Duke Street. Times had altered, however, and the persons most carefully debarred from engaging rooms were peers, and the sons, nephews, uncles, and brothers of peers. This was the cause of great pain to James Meakin, whose respect and admiration for the Peerage was as keen as that of his father, but he held that a man who let rooms was not necessarily a philanthropist.

It was in this house in Duke Street—the very name of which was inspiring—that young James Meakin served his apprenticeship. He waited upon the Army, the Navy, the Diplomatic Service, and finally upon Sir William Hutton, into whose permanent service he went upon the death of the elder Meakin.

There was no need for him to have entered into the service of anyone. His grandfather had left several thousand pounds to his father, and his father had left double that amount of thousands. If he had chosen, Meakin could have set up in Jermyn Street as a commission agent, worn

a white bowler hat, brown uppers to his boots,
yellow gloves and a well-cut suit of pepper and
salt, attended race meetings and hobnobbed with
the well-bred, scrupulous gentlemen who haunt
race-courses. He, too, could have been made
the subject of a cartoon in *Vanity Fair*, and if
he had kept a steady head, would, no doubt,
have eventually become possessed of a fine old
country house, a wife with much hair and a loud
voice, and servants of his own.

Heredity was, however, too strong for him.
He invested his money, and followed the noble
and remunerative calling of a gentleman's servant
with all the imagination, silence, tact, and diplo-
macy of his grandfather and his father.

Certainly the fact that, unlike the former
Meakins, he was in the service of a mere baronet,
who only had one country house and a small
place in Park Street, gave him occasional twinges
of regret. He was, however, an observant
person, and he comforted himself with the assurance that at any rate a baronet paid his wages
regularly, had no intention of going bankrupt,
was married to a gentlewoman, and so did not
ask him to put up with the vulgarity and in-
solence of a wife from the Gaiety Theatre.

Meakin knew Sir William Hutton as well as Vardon knows his brassie. He had made a close, perfectly accurate study of every one of his master's characteristics, moods, likes and dislikes. He therefore knew precisely how far to go with him and what to say at the proper moment. For all that he was attached to Hutton and admired him. If he had been born on the same social level as Hutton he would have made him his friend, although he would, in that case, have given him several pieces of his mind. It would take a novelist several pages to do full justice to Hutton's contradictory character. Two words were all that Meakin needed. When asked by an intimate friend to describe Sir William Hutton, he replied, with a faint wink, that he was " hot stuff."

He entered the room with the toast-rack at that precise moment because he had been listening outside the door.

CHAPTER III

HE was followed by a maid who carried some just cooked eggs. The toast and the eggs were placed quietly upon the table, and the man and woman left the room as silently as they had entered it.

"Besides," continued Mrs. Hay, as though there had been no interruption, "it is not quite fair to your old friend, who happens to be my husband. This toast is hot."

Hutton had made full use of Meakin's entrance. He had perfected an expression of iciness and politeness that would have done credit to Charles Hawtrey.

"Thanks," he said. "Rippin' weather."

Viola adopted his tone. "Yes, quite delightful for the time of year."

Hutton melted. "I knew you'd say that," he chuckled. "I say, Vi, have you ever done anythin' to your hair?"

"If you mean have I ever had it dyed, no, certainly not. Why?"

"The reason I asked—forgive personalities —is that its exquisite naturalness suggests artificiality. It's wonderful stuff. I never saw your eyes look so enticin' before, either."

"An egg?"

"Oh, bother. I mean yes, please." Hutton took the one Viola held out, and again his fingers touched hers. "By Jove, how soft and electrical."

" Yes," replied Mrs. Hay, " they're quite clever eggs."

Hutton threw himself back into his chair petulantly. " Oh, Lord," he said, " you *are* in a rummy mood this morning."

" Are you golfing to-day ? " asked Mrs. Hay, rising.

" Oh, I'll do whatever you're goin' to do."

Hutton rose also and stood silent for a moment with a look of almost fatuous admiration on his well-cut, sunburned face. " The sun's settin' your hair alight," he added. " It blazes like a beacon. *Do* be kind and give me just one."

Hutton was a tall man, as men go, but Mrs. Hay, as she stood eye to eye with him, appeared to be but the shade of an inch shorter. She ran her finger lightly and interestedly from button to button on his coat, and spoke slowly, with an effortless, musical drawl.

" My dear, impetuous, and transparent William," she said, " I'm no prude, but I have a great respect for the feelings of the servants. You see, they know that you are my husband's best friend, and they are very touchy on these points."

The sulky line round Hutton's mouth showed

plainly. "You're precious cautious about no-thin', all of a sudden. You shouldn't have let me kiss you if you're goin' to freeze me every time I come near you. What on earth's the world comin' to if a man can't be chummy with his pal's wife ? "

Mrs. Hay put her hands behind her, tilted her rounded chin, and looked at Hutton through her eyelashes.

" What would you say, my friend, if you caught my husband kissing your wife ? "

" I should say, ' Good luck, old man. Enjoy yourself,' " he replied airily. " But then, you see, he never would, y' know."

" Why not ? "

" Simply because my wife is not that type of woman."

Viola's voice would have cut a diamond. " I *beg* your pardon ? "

Hutton realised his hopeless mistake. " I mean to say that she don't kiss," he said pre-cipitately. " It don't appeal to her."

" How do you know that it appeals to me ? "

" It's all too jolly obvious that it don't," he said, with a cunning mixture of despair and desire.

His tone did its work. Viola recovered her

temper. " Is it, Billy dear ? " she asked softly, tilting her face forward ever so slightly.

With an exclamation of joy, Hutton put his hands on her shoulders.

There was a discreet cough. Meakin glided into the room.

" I thought I saw an earwig on your shoulder," said Hutton. " It's all right though." He threw a look at Meakin's expressionless face that contained the concentrated essence of a curse.

" Thanks so much," said Viola. " But I don't agree with you. I think the greens here are excellent."

Meakin was filling a match-holder with long, thick wooden matches. " They're pretty good as far as they go," said Hutton, watching Meakin and waiting to catch his eye. " But the rough is appalling ! more like the courses round London."

The little comedy amused Viola thoroughly. " I have never played over the London courses," she said. " How did you like West Drayton ? "

Hutton could barely control his temper. " West Drayton ? Oh, it's as flat as a board and by no means easy. Steaming hot mostly too."

" Yes, I suppose so."

Viola's laughing eyes and Meakin's quiet application to his unnecessary job were too much for Hutton's hot temper.

" What the devil are you doin', Meakin ? " he cried suddenly.

Meakin straightened up with slightly raised eyebrows. " Refilling the match-boxes, Sir William."

" Silly rot ! "

" Oh, I am so glad," said Viola. " I hunted everywhere for a match last night."

Hutton threw her a glance of appeal and irritation. Meakin returned to his work and Viola to her small talk.

" I've never wanted to play near London, but I'm awfully keen to go round Sunningdale. I suppose you know Sunningdale well ? "

" Yes," snapped Hutton. " I've often played there. Oh, damn ! " He twisted round upon Meakin. " Who told you to do this ? You ought to know by this time that I never permit anybody to fill these things. For endless years I've done it myself. Don't you remember ? "

Meakin thought for a moment. " Yes, I do remember, Sir William. I'm extremely sorry."

" Well, don't let me have to speak to you about it again."

" Very good, sir."

Meakin turned on his heel and walked noiselessly towards the door.

Hutton thought they they were alone again. " I say, Vi," he said, " did you ever in your life——"

Viola placed a finger upon her lip.

Hutton wheeled round. There was Meakin carefully arranging the curtains.

" What are you playing at now, Meakin ? You fill match-boxes and puff curtains. Can't you find anythin' to do ? "

Meakin looked hurt.

" You know we're very short-handed here. Surely to goodness they can find you somethin' to do in the kitchen ? "

Meakin bowed and moved up to the door. " Shall I leave the matches here, Sir William ? " he asked.

" What ?   Oh, yes, anywhere, anywhere."

" I have placed them against the naked foot of the little statue of Physic, Sir William."

Hutton glared at the man, and then glared at the door that closed behind him.   " Cunnin' scoundrel ! " he said.   " He's been with me goodness knows how long, or I'd sack him."

Viola laughed a little and held out her hand. "My hat, please," she said.

Hutton picked up a cunning arrangement of straw and roses. "Fool," he muttered. "I don't know what's come over the modern servant. He never used to barge in at the wrong moment. Let's get out of here. He must have had his eye screwed to the keyhole. Let's go where we were yesterday. We can't be overlooked. Buck up, Vi."

"Dear Billy, don't bustle me. The day is in front of us." She ran a long pin dangerously through the hat.

"You're driving me crazy," said Hutton.

A second pin followed the first to the accompaniment of a rippling laugh. "Poor Peg. I wonder if she cares the least little bit for you now, Billy?"

"Cares for me? Peg?" There was an almost incredulous note of surprise in Hutton's voice. "I should think she does. But she's a sensible little woman. She gives me plenty of line."

"Yes, you'd break it if she didn't," said Viola. "Still, I think she rather underrates the attractions of other women."

"Oh, but she knows me," replied Hutton. "I flirt a bit, of course, but there's never any danger in it."

Viola turned. Her beautiful slim figure was thrown up against the dark wainscot of the little hall. She looked like a drawing by Balliol Salmon.

"And now, Billy?" she asked. "Can you grow fond of me without any danger?"

Hutton sprang forward. "Danger be hanged!" he said. "You're divine."

Viola slipped away. "You do it extremely well," she laughed. "You must have lots of practice."

Before he could speak again, Viola put her finger on the tail of a tortoise bell. It set up a loud ringing.

"Oh, Lord," cried Hutton, "don't bring that beggar back!"

"But I want him."

Meakin opened the door.

"You will see that the second breakfast is ready on Major Hay's return, please," she said.

"Very good, madame."

"Are my clubs clean?" asked Hutton.

"Quite clean, Sir William. Shall I——"

" No. That's all, thanks."

Almost before Meakin had left the room Hutton turned to Viola triumphantly. " I'd have laid odds on my being right," he said. " Meakin was spyin'."

" How do you know ? "

" My dear child, there is always a draught through a keyhole. That beggar's eye's blood-shot. I say, Vi."

" Well ? "

Hutton touched his tie and lowered his voice. A sudden new air of solemnity and mystery had come upon him.

" I hate subterfuge and cunnin' and all that. One doesn't go in for 'em, of course. But look here, I don't think we'd better be seen goin' out together again."

" Good gracious, why not ? "

" I dunno," said Hutton. " We don't want gossip. Besides, Archie may turn jealous."

Viola scoffed. " Archie jealous ! Oh ho, that's gorgeous."

If Hutton had not been so much occupied with his own line of thought he might have detected something in Viola's remark that would have conveyed a distinct impression that the fact that Hay was not jealous was a grievance. As it was he read into her remark something that piqued him.

" Think so ? " he replied. " Well, there *have* been stories about me, y' know."

" I'm making no aspersions on your well-known fascinations, my dear Billy. But the bare idea of Archie's being able to think of anything outside his own concerns shows how little you know of the man you know so well. Archie —jealous ! "

Hutton forgave her. " However, let's play the game. Let's remember that we are people of breeding. While I go for my pills you go upstairs for your handkerchief or something. Then you go out first, aimlessly, and I'll bustle down to the club-house ten minutes later and join you in our usual spot. Don't you think so ? "

" Very well," said Viola. " If it amuses you. Anyone would think that we were desperately in love."

Hutton caught her elbows. " We are," he said. " At least I am, and you're going to be. Desperately. The world would be very well lost for you."

"Oh, isn't that nice," said Viola, with mock delight. She freed herself and waved him away. "Go for your clubs, you humbug."

Hutton marched slowly to the door. Arrived there he turned. "Ah, you little know," he said solemnly. "You little know."

CHAPTER IV

VIOLA had the greatest difficulty to preserve a grave face while Hutton was indulging in his parting touch of temporarily sincere sentiment, delivered with an unconscious theatricalism that was irresistibly funny. But when he had made his exit her desire for laughter left her.

She threw back her mind over what had occurred at the breakfast-table. She saw herself deliberately setting out to draw the husband of the woman who was her closest and dearest friend into a strong flirtation. With a distinct loss of self-respect she saw herself playing with the feelings of a very good fellow—a little too egotistical perhaps, a little too self-indulgent certainly, not endowed with the highest form of intelligence, a good all-round sportsman who was not only extremely susceptible, but who had arrived at that time of life when a man who always has been very attractive to women begins to be afraid that he is losing some of his attractiveness.

She had permitted him to kiss her once, and by holding him off had made him more eager than ever to repeat the process. She knew Hutton well. She knew that although he had been, and would be always, an easy prey to any beautiful woman who chose to flatter him, he loved his wife devotedly. She knew that his definition of the word disloyalty was an elastic one, and that kissing, the saying of ardent and high-flown things, and the holding of hands surreptitiously were, according to him, mere ordinary pleasantries of a perfectly unobjectionable nature. She was quite sure that it would be impossible, so long as Peg Hutton remained interested in and kind to him, for Hutton to be really and indisputably disloyal.

Without hedging with the truth, she assured herself that Hutton did not attract her in the least. She never had found the susceptible type of man worth bothering about. He was too easy, too elementary. He started by being desperately in love, and gradually underwent the process of cooling off, instead of starting by being quite cool and slightly indifferent, and gradually becoming desperately in love.

Nevertheless, finding herself hopelessly dissatisfied with the relations between herself and her husband, whom she loved passionately, Viola was determined to carry out an experiment to the success of which Billy Hutton was necessary. She knew well enough that her husband loved her. He never would have married her if he had not, for he belonged to the type of man who loves and marries against his will. But she needed more than just to know that he loved her. She wanted, even after five years of married life, to be told so frequently. She resented with all her soul her husband's attitude of blissful content with things as they were. She was a woman of temperament, a woman whose vanity needed nourishment just as much as her body needed it ; a woman who nursed imaginary grievances, whose entire outlook was warped and darkened by a tactless remark into which she read a meaning utterly foreign to the one intended, and whose heart was made bitter by the remark, to which she had led up, remaining unspoken.

She was determined to give Archie Hay's com-

placency a rude shock by making him jealous.
She had, after much mental agony, deliberately
formulated a scheme to make Archie wake up to
the fact that it was easy to lose the woman whose
love he was so happy in having won. It was
she who found the golf cottage on the range of
downs behind Worthing ; it was she who suggested that Archie should ask his friend Hutton
to share it with him ; and it was she, and not
Hutton, who had started the flirtation.

They had been at the cottage for ten days.
During the whole of eight of these days Billy
had followed her about like a dog. She had
hoped that before this her scheme might have had
some effect. But it seemed to her that Peg was
merely mildly amused—and for this she was
thankful—and that Archie was just as com-
placent and self-satisfied as ever, which made her
very irritable.

CHAPTER V

As Viola crossed the small, square room that
was estate-agently called the hall, Archibald
Hay's tall, broad, wiry, muscular body blocked
the doorway. The peak of his cap was pulled

over one blue eye. His fair skin was the colour of brick-dust. Beneath his large, fair moustache there was a smile of ineffable content. He reeked gloriously of tobacco and turf.

He put a huge hand on Viola's shoulder and touched her chin with his moustache.

" Morning, little woman."

" Good morning."

" All right ? "

" Oh, quite, thanks."

" That's good." He gave her round arm a little squeeze, and nodded at her in a kindly, elderly way. Then he passed on, dropped into a chair, threw one long leg over the other, fished a well-crammed pouch out of one pocket and a pipe out of another.

" Well," he said, " I've done my duty, at any rate."

" Duty ? " echoed his wife.

" Well, a very excellent morning's work then."

Viola resisted the natural temptation to echo the word " work " as well. All that she did do was to stand where Hay had left her, with her arm still tingling with the remembrance of his perfunctory caress. And as she stood with a resolute lack of expression upon her beautiful almost Southern face, she looked at her husband with a curious examining glance. She found every inch of him to her utter satisfaction, but very bitterly, and with a rush of scalding tears to her eyes, she asked herself why just as easily he couldn't have kissed her and held her tight for a moment and told her how scrumptious she looked and how extremely young.

Only vaguely she realised that he was talking.

"By Jove, yes. It's true. One can live to be a hundred and still be without a glimmer of an idea of the science of the game. You'll hardly believe it, Vi, but do you know this? I've played golf—that is to say I've held clubs—for fifteen years, and I've only this very morning discovered the whole value of the mashie. What do you think of that?"

Viola found it impossible to prevent the suggestion of a sneer. "I agree with you," she replied. "It's a great day for England." Then she turned and made her way to the door with rather more hip play than was characteristic of her.

Hay was obviously puzzled. He watched her sharply, and as he watched he involuntarily scratched his chin.

" Got a headache, old girl ? " he asked.

" I ? Oh dear no. I'm almost too well ! "

Hay struck a match and lit his pipe expertly. " That's what I mean," he said slowly. " You're saying rather odd things this morning."

Viola shot out a staccato laugh.

" How can one be almost too well, I mean ? "

Just for a moment an overwhelming desire, a passionate longing swept over her to throw her arms round Hay's neck and pour out all her pent-up grievances before him once for all, to show him into what kind of dangerous temper his treatment was driving her, to confess what she had planned to do rather than entreat him to pursue a less self-satisfied course, and implore him to be different, to pander—if he liked to call it pandering—to her temperament, to treat her as though she were a very human being and not a wife, a certainty, a fixture, a thing won, an institution. And if she had allowed herself to do this, if she had ruthlessly and daringly ignored the thing in her that was called pride, the Hay-Hutton episode, as Meakin pleasantly designated it, would have ended here on a note of light comedy, and would not very nearly have developed into a sordid and miserable tragedy.

As it was she permitted what she called pride to win.

"I won't explain," she said. "You big, normal, Saxon sportsman mustn't be teased with psychological discussions on temperament, especially the female temperament. . . . What are you doing to-day?"

"Ah," said Hay, now in his depth, "I've mapped out a heavy day's work. As soon after breakfast as I can get away, the pro is going to help me to cure a slight tendency to slice. At eleven-thirty I'm booked to play a return match with a man called Grant-Duffie—very hot stuff—I lunch with him at the club; and in the afternoon he and I have a four-ball match with old Wedderburn and Alex Maclean, members here, both very useful."

"And after dinner?"

"After dinner I'm going to attack Braid's new book seriously."

Viola hesitated on the threshold. "You wouldn't care to scratch your appointment with the pro and come for a walk with me?"

"My dear child, I should love it; but really I must *not* waste time."

"Thank you," she said.

" You understand that, don't you ? " asked Hay, not quite sure if there was not something a little short in his wife's reply.

" Perfectly."

" What are *you* going to do ? "

Viola answered without giving the matter an instant's consideration, " Oh, yawn, eat, smoke, sleep—kill time in the usual way."

" That's right, dear," said Hay. " I'm glad you're putting in such a good time."

Viola examined her husband closely. Finding no vestige of chaff or sarcasm, nothing, in fact, but his usual good-tempered cheeriness about him, she turned on her heel once more, shrugged her shoulders ever so slightly, and left the hall.

Hay took out a small pair of scissors and pared his nails earnestly. And as he pared he whistled.

He told himself with a touch of excitement, that the mashie was now worth half a stroke to him, and, in order to make certain that this was a fact, went carefully over his morning's practice again mentally, putting himself back metaphorically into the same stances, gripping the club in the same way, and playing the ball in the same wristy manner. He even went a step beyond this.   He played some of the strokes that he was looking forward to play in his match with Grant-Duffie, imagining that his drive and his brassie would take him within a mashie shot of several of the shorter holes.   He then, with great care, played the shots as he had played them before breakfast, and had, in imagination, the infinite satisfaction of laying them dead on the green.

Hutton discovered him paring his nails and whistling quietly.

" Hullo, old cock," said Hutton.

" Hullo, Billy ! " said Hay.

Hutton filled his cigarette-case from a large silver box.

" Do any good, old man ? "

Hay looked up with a smile.   His teeth were strong and good.   He looked extraordinarily boyish and ingenuous.

" Did lots of good," he replied, " thanks.   I stuck to the mashie for three hours—short approaches.   All right now."

" Good for you, b'jove."

" Yes, it . . . it makes life much more comfortable.   I was telling Vi.   She was tremendously interested."

Hutton knew that Hay thought so.   He never

said anything that he did not believe. " Was
she ? " he said dryly.

" Yes. She's an ideal sportsman's wife, is Vi."
Hay got up, stumped over to the open window,
and knocked out his pipe. Then he sat on the
arm of a chair and loaded the hot pipe again
slowly. " My dear man," he continued, with a
characteristic touch of sententiousness, " the
whole thing comes to this. A man may dedicate
the best years of his life to golf, and go to his
grave a novice. You playing to-day ? "

" Rather ! " replied Hutton emphatically.
" What am I here for ? "

Hay hesitated. " You're not going to . . . to
hang about with the women—with Vi ? "

" Good Lord, no, my dear chap ! I've not got
softenin' of the brain yet."

" No," said Hay, " but you've not played with
me or the other fellows for three days."

" Givin' you a chance to catch up, old man,"
replied Hutton airily.

Hay was a scrupulously honourable man.
He was also shrewd, just, and, for a soldier, intelligent. He was also strangely unsuspicious,
but he was totally devoid of a sense of humour.

" My dear old man," he said warmly, " how awf'ly nice of you. Well, I must go and do a wash before breakfast."

Hutton watched his friend go out. He admired his straight back and immense shoulders. He envied the complete absence of superfluous flesh, the close-cropped hair with its natural kink. And as he watched his conscience gave him one small twinge. Archie was so easy to humbug . . . and Vi was not difficult to kiss.

He then went to the window, saw Mrs. Hay gliding gracefully over the springy turf silhouetted against the wide expanse of cloudless sky, gazed after her for a moment with delight and appreciation, switched himself back into a condition of fatuous sentimentality, and waited with impatience for what he conceived to be the right moment to follow. And as he put a relay of matches into his box he sang softly about that night in June, that lovely night, that night of nights.

His wife came in at this moment, looking as sweet and fresh as a primrose.

CHAPTER VI

" SURELY not my errant Bill, my wandering Willie ! Oh, Willie, we have missed you."

Her voice was as sweet and fresh as her appearance. She wore something soft and white. Her face and hands were tanned, and her hair, where the sun had caught it, had gone into straw-coloured patches. The whites of her grey eyes were exquisitely white, and there were several tantalising freckles on her short, straight nose.

" Missed me ? When ? "

" Every day—all day. You and Viola——"

Hutton held up a hand with quiet dignity. " Please," he said.

" Oh, I beg your pardon, dear William," said Peg. " I forgot that this is one of your serious episodes about which one mustn't joke. Why aren't you out with her this morning as usual ? Oh, don't say that you've quarrelled ! "

Hutton regarded his wife coldly. " I haven't the remotest notion what you mean," he said.

Peg smiled.

It had the usual effect. " I say," cried Hutton, " what a rippin' kit."

" Like it ? Does it suit me ? "

" It don't matter what you wear, Peggy. You always look the sweetest thing breathing."

Peg tilted her head to one side. " Billy," she

said, " you've done something that you're afraid
I shall find out."

" Don't be foolish," said Hutton. " But, look
here, I've been wanting to speak to you."

Peg sat down in a comfortable chair, fluffed
out her frock, and folded her hands in her lap.
" I thought so. Well, confess."

" Oh, it's nothing of that sort. What I mean
is that you oughtn't to leave me so much alone.
It's not wise."

Not the vaguest suggestion of a twinkle appeared in Peg's eyes. She retained an air of deliciously sympathetic gravity.

" You still feel the need of a nurse, Billy ? "
she asked.

Hutton dashed a finger along his moustache.
" Be serious. I mean, if you must have it, you're
gettin' into the habit of neglectin' me. It hurts."

Gravity had to go. Peg doubled up with
laughter. " Oh, Billy, Billy," she said, with tears
in her eyes, " life would be very dull without you."

But Hutton, like Hay, had, luckily, not been
cursed with the sense of humour. He possessed
nothing but the sense of the ridiculous, which
has no more relation to the sense of humour than
a tooth-brush has to a looking-glass.

" You do love me still, don't you ? " he asked pathetically.

Peg pulled down his head and placed a kiss upon his forehead. " You funny old thing," she said tenderly. " Now run away and amuse yourself, dear."

Hutton drew himself up, squared his shoulders, and took a long breath. " I shall live on that all day," he announced, with genuine sincerity.

" How economical," said Peg.

" I shall play as a really happy man."

" With Viola to help you, dear ? "

" Oh, yes," he replied airily. " Vi will be there. She's . . . she's . . . well, as a matter of fact I think she needs brightenin' up—poor old Vi."

" Oh, does she ?   Poor old Vi."

Hutton lit a cigarette. " Of course," he continued, " I don't want to assume virtues I don't possess, or any rot of that sort, but when a woman wants brightenin' up one ought to do what little one can for her.   At least, that's my idea.   What ? "

" Of course, Billy dear.   Very, very kind of you.   In fact, it's just like you."

Hutton threw his wife a look of profound admiration. " By Jove, how well you understand me, don't you ? "

" Through and through," replied Peg, with a tiny laugh.

She received a kiss. " Darlin' old girl."

" Dear old boy."

Hutton straightened his tie and ran his hand down the back of his head.

" I wish you were comin' with me," he said.

" Tell me where to find you and I'll join you."

The reply was unexpected and a little awkward. " Will you, will you really ? Oh, that's great." Hutton went towards the door, stopped, and turned. " Er . . . but don't you think it's . . . I mean, I mean, you'd better not. You'll be happier here with all your busy little ways. Well, so long, darling."

Peg rose. " I'll see you off, Billy."

" Oh, no, don't bother."

" Bother ? What bosh."

She took his arm and they went out together.

CHAPTER VII

WHEN asked by elderly ladies if she was quite happy, Peg Hutton always replied, and replied with strict truthfulness, that she had every reason to be happy, as her marriage was a great success.

She and Hutton had been married for seven years. Not once during that time had there been anything approaching a quarrel. It was a big thing to be able to boast about. There are two thousand five hundred and fifty-five days in seven years, and there had been many moments during sixty per cent. of these days when any other woman married to William Hutton would have quarrelled certainly. But Peg, wiser than her sisters, had not permitted herself to be led to the altar and tied for life—unless she chose to make herself, and had the proper grounds for making herself and her set, the topic of discussion for the readers of the *Daily Telegraph* and all the other necessary daily papers—to this man in the first blush of mutual attraction.

She fell in love with Hutton and immediately vetoed all allusion to marriage. She saw as much of him as her daily list of events allowed. She studied him more closely than the wise man who is going to live in France studies Chardenal, for exactly the same reason. She made herself acquainted with all his good qualities, and with

as many of his bad ones as possible. Having
done this she did a little sum. She put his good
qualities on one line and his bad ones beneath it,
and deducted them. If his good qualities had
not exceeded his bad ones by three points she
would have taken the first opportunity of telling
him, in her peculiarly charming way, that although
she would not marry him on any account whatever, she would be quite delighted to number
him among her friends. As it was she married
him, for she was one of those almost unique
women who do not expect any human creature to
be perfect so long as he remains human. She
told herself that he was extremely vain. But
she added that he was delightfully good-natured.
She placed against his tendency to blaze up, an
instinct for sportsmanship that was characteristically English. He sulked when he felt that he
was injured, but he was genuinely affectionate.
Any pretty woman could twist him round her
finger, but his heart was only large enough to
contain one woman—herself. It was impossible
to drive him, but extremely simple to make him
follow.

During his term of probation Peg never acted.
She was, when with him, strictly natural. She

honestly permitted him to see her as she was, and not as she wished him to see her. She treated him before she married him as she intended to treat him after she had married him. The consequence was that when these two left the altar, for better or for worse, both of them knew the best and the worst of each other and were content. They did not make the fatal mistake of starting upon a honeymoon with rose-coloured glasses on their noses. Neither had placed the other upon a pedestal, which is apt to be a very trying thing for a human being to pose upon for any length of time with comfort. As there were no romantic illusions there could be no frightful disillusions. In their case, therefore, marriage was a legalised friendship, a partnership in the best sense of the word, a collaboration of lives by two people who intended to make the most of life—a combination that was bound to be successful.

Naturally enough, having quickly discovered that Hutton possessed no sense of humour, Peg did not let him know by the vaguest hint or suggestion that he had been on probation. Hutton would have been extremely hurt. He would have called her calculating and unromantic. No argu-

ment would have made him see that any marriage
rushed blindly into without careful and sympathetic calculation on both sides, and with a
stern disregard of romance, must lead to the
Divorce Court, the chambers of the family solicitor, or to an existence made bitter by constant
wrangles, an innumerable amount of back-handed
insinuations, jealousy, discontent, dislike, armed
neutrality.

Although infinitely more intelligent and quick
than her husband, Peg never once allowed herself
to commit the egregious fault of teaching. Nor
did she ever, being endowed with a quite wonderful intuition, convey the impression that she
knew, or thought that she knew, that she was
the superior person. All that she did do was
quietly to set an example. She had her own
way in everything by appearing to give way to
him, very frequently pulling him gently away
from the object to which she very greatly desired
him to go. Tact was the keynote of her success,
tact tempered with sunny good temper.

She was an energetic, busy woman, with many
hobbies and occupations, but she always had
plenty of time to give to her husband. She did
not only make herself look charming for others.

She made herself look her most charming for her husband. She had no company manners. She was her best self at home. Having been born under a lucky star, she was an optimist. She woke up to find life a very delightful thing, the world a very charming place ; and as she never was punished by a bad liver, or a bad back, or bad headaches, as she possessed a sufficiency of money, very pleasant surroundings, and inherited the gift of filling up every moment of her day, she saw no reason why life should not continue to be a very delightful thing and the world made even more charming than she found it.

All of which goes to prove that Lady Hutton was a quite exceptionally sensible and desirable little woman.

CHAPTER VIII

When Meakin came back to the hall for the purpose of giving Stanner, the maid, a hand with the second breakfast he was chuckling. He took the precaution to shut the door leading to the staircase before he condescended to enter into conversation with the girl, with whom he had been walking out for some little time.

Stanner was a pretty child not yet twenty, the

daughter of the housekeeper at Beauly, Hutton's place in Kent. She had been carefully brought up.

" Ho, ho ! " laughed Meakin, as he removed the plates to a tray on the dresser, " he's a great boy, and no mistake."

" I think he's a very wicked man," said Stanner.

" That's why he's so popular." Meakin had a great and fatal facility for easy repartee. He began to laugh again. " I cut the kiss in half though. I timed it to the second each time. Oh, wouldn't he have called me some pretty choice names if he'd had the chance ! He'll have forgotten when he sees me next."

Stanner looked frightened and horrified. " Well, my mind's made up," she said. " I shall tell her ladyship."

Meakin drew up suddenly. Every muscle of his body had tightened under the shock. " Well," he said, " your ignorance is your only excuse for such a threat. My good girl, you must never interfere with the pastimes of the best people."

" Pastimes ! " echoed the girl, through rising tears. " How do we know what it's going to lead to ? "

Meakin touched his collar. " Being human

ourselves, and having spent some years in a cultivated atmosphere, I presoom we can guess."

They were relaying the table. Meakin placed the knives and forks with an air of cunning, and he cast his eye on the worn crest upon the spoons warmly.

" The way the master was behavin' was simply shockin'," continued Stanner.

" Eh, my dear ? Ah yes, there's no doubt about his having descended from the old crusaders. He's my bow idil of a mash."

" That may be," replied the girl agitatedly. " But if you ask me, there'll be a fuss before long."

Meakin shivered. " A fuss ? . . . Do remember that we are not in Bayswater."

" All the same, the Major don't show it, but he's gettin' very touchy at the way they're carryin' on."

" Major Hay comes of one of the best families," replied Meakin, now on his dignity. " Certainly it is Scots, but it has been settled in Mayfair long enough to become civilised."

Stanner was a girl of some character. She stood in extreme awe of Meakin, of whose long connection with the aristocracy she knew, and of whose more than comfortable income she had been told frequently. But she had been a church worker at Old Trenton, and would be again, and had very old-fashioned ideas of right and wrong.

" Anyway," she repeated pluckily, " I shall tell her ladyship."

Meakin sniffed. " If you do," he said quietly, " I shall have to ask you to return my engagement ring and keeper, to say nothing of them handkerchiefs and stockings. You are an average female adult and they will fit another."

Tears streamed down Stanner's pretty face. " I can't help it," she said through her sobs, " it's my duty."

She caught up the loaded tray and made for the door.

Meakin opened it for her coldly. " When a woman begins to talk about her duty," he remarked to the world at large, " the Lord help us."

Hay came into the hall. " Morning," said he.

" Good morning, sir," said Meakin.

" Why have you only laid for two? Have Sir William and Mrs. Hay had breakfast?"

" Just finished, sir."

" Oh!"

Hay went over to the window. He looked uncomfortable and perturbed.

"Will you take your breakfast at once, sir, or wait for her ladyship?"

"What? Oh, I'll wait for her ladyship, of course."

"Very good, sir."

Before Meakin left the hall he darted a searching, curious look at the Major, and asked himself whether, after all, Stanner was not right when she said, in her atrocious village manner, that Major Hay was getting touchy.

Hay remained at the window. Evidently his thoughts were not particularly pleasant, for he began to pull his eyebrows.

"I say," he called out suddenly. "Meakin." Meakin came to the door.

"Sir?"

"Oh, by the way, has Mrs. Hay gone out?"

"Madam went down to the club-house about twenty minutes ago, sir. Sir William went out to join her."

"To play?"

"Sir William took his clubs, sir, but I see that he left all his Challengers behind."

"Thank you."

Meakin bowed and went.

"Damn!" said Hay.

CHAPTER IX

" I BEG your pardon, Archie ? "

Hay turned and forced a laugh. " I beg yours, again and again."

" Don't mind me," said Peg. " But why did you make use of that harmless, necessary word ? Anything wrong ? "

" Oh, no, no. No. I—I understood from Vi that she was going to be busy in the house, and I find that she . . ."

" Has gone out with Billy ? "

" Yes, but it doesn't matter, of course. I'm glad. Had a good night ? "

" Splendid," said Peg. " How did you get on ? "

" Pretty well, thanks. I am better with my wrists."

" That's good," said Peg, with enthusiasm. " The mashie *is* so important, isn't it ? "

Meakin came in followed by Stanner. Both carried hot dishes.

" Here's breakfast," added Peg. " You must be starving." She sat down.

So did Hay. " I was ten minutes ago," he

said. "My appetite seems to have lost its edge."

His tone of depression caught Peg's quick ears. "Something's happened," she thought. What she said was, "Wait till the aroma of this omelette reaches you."

"What kind of omelette is it?"

"Insular. Egg, egg, and again egg."

"I think I will," said Hay.

"Of course you will." Peg made a long arm with a plate. "Coffee, don't you? You needn't wait, Meakin. We'll look after ourselves. . . . One quarter milk and two lumps of sugar?"

Meakin and Stanner faded away.

The rally of question and answer stopped. Hay and Lady Hutton looked more comfortable and became more confidential.

"How well you know my eccentricities," said Hay, smiling.

"Well, you see," repeated Peg, pouring out coffee with her pretty head on one side, "eight breakfasts . . . eight dinners . . . and seven teas running alone with the same man give a woman an excellent opportunity of getting to know his little ways—almost as excellent as though she were married to him."

"More excellent," said Hay, with a slightly injured air.

Peg made a second mental note. "Oh," she said to herself. "I see. He's at last beginning to notice the Billy-Viola episode! . . . Well, what are your plans for to-day?"

"I play as long as possible. Then I study. Pretty busy. What would you like to do?"

Peg gave a laugh. "I shall do what I don't like and answer some letters."

Archie pushed forward the butter. "I'm afraid you'll find it a bit dull this morning. Viola, I fancy——"

"Oh, I wouldn't disturb Viola for worlds. When I string myself up to the heroic act of writing letters I like to be quite alone with a dictionary."

"It's very kind of you to put it like that," replied Hay.

"Kind?" echoed Peg. "How?"

"Well, Viola is your friend, and, after all, you share this cottage with us in order to be with her."

"The exquisite country was somewhere in the back of my head."

Hay began to dig holes in the salt. Wherefore Peg knew that he was in need of sympathy.

"Honestly," he began. "I've been—not worried, because, as you know, I'm not a worrying chap, quite un-jealous, and all that—and, of course, I trust Vi implicitly, but——"

"Well?"

Hay hesitated. "But I've been wondering whether you have been thinking that it's rather queer form that . . . that we should be left to entertain each other quite so much."

"Not the least bit in the world, believe me," Peg assured him. "Besides, you see, I know Billy."

"Of course, but——"

"He needs constant amusement and I love him to be amused, because it saves me the trouble. I'm sure Vi doesn't mind. In fact, she rather likes it. She places entertaining among the fine arts. And so she's happy, Billy's happy, I'm happy, and you're happy—at least, I suppose you are?"

Hay was too emphatic. "Of course—of course I am. Rather. I should think so. I was only thinking about you. I was nervous—hardly nervous—perhaps a little afraid that you——"

" Well ? "

" Might—well, to be honest, might misunderstand the position. That's what I mean, Peg."

Peg knew that her suspicions were well founded. " I'm afraid you're jealous of Billy," she said.

" I'm afraid I am," replied Hay. " I wasn't until just now. It's just got hold of me. I hate myself for it."

" Well, I can assure you," said Peg, " that there is no need for jealousy. Billy and Viola are indulging in a quite commonplace flirtation."

" Commonplace ? When they've been inseparable every day since we've been here ? "

" Certainly. I repeat, from a ripe knowledge of both of them, commonplace and to be expected."

Hay looked immensely astonished. He was right out of his depth. " To be expected ? But why ? "

" Well, I'll tell you," said Peg, putting her elbows on the table. " About once a year a husband gets bored—not exactly with his wife, but with his surroundings."

" I don't," ran in Hay.

" I know you don't. I'm talking about husbands as an Institution. And about once a year the wife frets at the touch of the hand on the curb—not the husband's hand exactly, but the hand of her surroundings. You see the husband has a way, however really affectionate and faithful he may be, of taking things for granted. He is perfectly well aware that his wife is the only woman in the world, so why constantly call attention to it ? "

" Exactly. My point. Why ? "

" Ah," continued Peg, raising one finger. " Ah, but madame the wife *likes* the attention called, constantly, continuously, vociferously. This is the little rift within the lute. And at this moment the *other* man comes upon the scene. Obviously he possesses, for the time being, every virtue the husband lacks, because he not only admires her, but—mark this !—*he tells her so.*"

" Like his beastly cheek," said Hay. " Well, what does the husband do then ? "

" The wise husband allows the little flirtation."

" Allows it ? " cried Hay loudly.

" Certainly. It bores the wife to tears in about a month, because you see it takes just that time for her to find out how unlike her husband this other man is, and it is always to the other man's disadvantage. When the incident is over——"

" Well," asked Hay eagerly.

" The wise husband sets back the calendar to the honeymoon, and 'God's in His heaven, all's right with the world.'"

Hay pushed back his chair and rose. And as he rose he gave a big laugh.

" By Jove," he said, with all the depression gone from his face, " you're a wonderful little woman. How the dickens do you know these things ? "

" Observation, dear man," replied Peg dryly, " and—and experience."

" But, hang it, I've had heaps of experience. Do you mean to accuse me of possessing no observation ? "

" My dear Archie," replied Peg with a delicious touch of sententiousness, " no amount of observation ever enables a man to understand a woman."

" Good Lord, why not ? "

" Because a man looks at a woman through the strongest magnifying glass that's invented. That, unfortunately, confines him to the surface. Now a woman applies the X-Rays of intuition and *sees right through*."

Hay laughed. "It sounds all right," he said. "And so there's no need for me to worry, eh?"

"Not in the least. You see, according to your argument, Billy has just as much right to be jealous of you as you have to be jealous of him."

"Jealous of me?" Hay's voice became shrill with amazement. "Good Lord, why?"

Peg bent forward and sank her voice. "Haven't we been together since we came here, day after day, meal after meal? How do you know that he isn't holding his head under the impression that you are madly in love with me?"

Hay was too simple a man to understand the value of flattery. "In love with you? Ho, ho!"

"Other men have managed it, you know," remarked Peg blandly.

Tact came to Hay's rescue. "The wonder to me is that I'm not one of them." His voice became grave. "The trouble is that all my heart is Viola's. There is no room in it for any other woman."

"A good thing too, my friend," laughed Peg. "A man who has room in his heart for more than one woman at a time goes through bankruptcy or divorce. Are you happier now?"

" Much. A thousand thanks. I don't often screw up my courage to talk about the things I feel deeply—I wish I could—I wish I had confided in you at once. I can't tell you what tortures I endured just now when I suddenly realised that Vi and Billy had slipped out together again, for the ninth day ! "

" But surely you trust Viola ? "

" Good heavens, yes ! But you're not jealous, and so you can't imagine the sort of hideous things that rush through a jealous brain."

" I never suspected you of jealousy, Archie," said Peg.

" No one ever has. I'd never till to-day suspected myself. It's rather humiliating."

" However, I've blown it away, eh ? "

" Yes, thank heaven, you have—heaven, and your dose of common sense."

" If common sense were sold in bottles, my dear," said Peg, " there would be no coughs, no liver complaints, no murders, and no broken hearts. Bags I the writing-table."

She ran to it and sat down.

" By all means," said Hay lightly, beaming at her. " Pocket the whole cottage. I'm going to putt." He marched to the door.

" Shall I tell you what I think would be a far more useful thing to do ? Go after Billy and Vi, and flirt desperately with her yourself."

" That's a rattling good idea," said Hay.

" Well, of course. It's mine, you know."

" Yes, it's a great idea. I'll get them to come back to luncheon, and we'll be a jolly foursome. It'll be like old days again."

" Only eight days old," said Peg.

" Looking back, they've seemed like eight months to me."

Peg gave a little laugh. " I *must* have been heavy on the hand. God bless you, dear friend."

" God bless *you*, dear friend," said Hay earnestly.

CHAPTER X

WHENEVER Hay felt at peace with the world he always began to whistle a dolorous, tum-te-tum waltz tune that was popular in the early eighties. And as there were very few moments when he did not feel at peace with the world, it goes without saying that the people who lived under his roof or anywhere within earshot of his rather ugly but extremely comfortable house knew that waltz tune very well.

The fact that Hay was always, with an exception here and there, at peace with the world, had, however, nothing to do with the world, but everything to do with Hay. Like all men who are six foot three, he was not a creature of brain, but of muscle. He had no more imagination than a plate, and it was therefore impossible to expect of him any such uncomfortable gifts as psychology, creativeness, or invention.

His was a mathematical brain. He was intensely accurate. He was a good organiser. He had a retentive memory, and was uncommonly useful with his hands. His industry was remarkable. He filled up every moment of his day. He devoted all his waking hours to games. He called this working in the true English manner. He was therefore a fine cricketer, and one of the best real tennis players of his day. At golf he was becoming every day more useful. He was a crack shot, an expert fisherman, and he played bridge infinitely well, though without a suggestion of originality or daring.

As an ex-officer of cavalry he rode well, but being quite unhorsy he played only a fair game of polo. Racing bored him insufferably. So, indeed, did anything else at which he was bound to be a spectator.

He was an able soldier who inevitably would have become a general. He was a master of detail. His gift of organisation won him a staff appointment during the South African War and his majority. Although he had no notion of how to inspire the affection of his men, his consideration for them gained him their respect, and his sportsmanship as well as his great height and physique their admiration.

At the termination of the war, however, he left the service in order to devote himself to the serious things of life—fishing, cricket, golf, and tennis. He found that it was impossible to do justice to these things and remain a soldier. Then it was that he met Viola Pilkington. To his intense annoyance, being a born bachelor, he found that he was in love with her. The fact that another person entered into his plans upset his arrangements considerably. Finding that however much he wanted to play golf, tennis, or to fish, he wanted even more to be with or near Viola, he gave the matter a week's irritable consideration and decided that marriage would put an end to a position that had become intolerable.

He made his honeymoon a combination of pleasure and business by taking the opportunity afforded by a two months' tour on the Continent of playing over the best of the French golf courses. The honeymoon over, he very gladly returned home to take up the business of his life. Any time that could justly be spared from his cricket, shooting, fishing, tennis, and golf he gave cheerfully to his wife.

If at any time during the five years of his, to him, completely satisfactory and successful married life his wife had accused him of selfishness he would have been thunderstruck.

Viola made no such accusation aloud. Indeed, in all these five years she did not accuse him of selfishness even to herself during any of her lonely unoccupied hours. When it was possible she went with him on his cricket tours, his fishing expeditions, and his golf holidays, and continued to regard him as a hero, a man who could do no wrong. She was obsessed with his bigness. She adored his handsome face. She was awed by his overwhelming ego. In her eyes he was a king among men. When, as was natural, her enthusiasm for his games gradually cooled, and she began to see nothing of him from breakfast until dinner, she was lonely, but not miserable. Was she not married to the man to whom every other woman in the world would give her head for a smile?

So great and passionate was her love for Hay that for five years of her life Viola forgot herself and her temperament. Her vanity was satisfied by the possession of Hay.

All went well until one Canterbury week. She and Hay went, as usual, to stay with old Sir Hugh de Brissac. Hay was playing for the County eleven, and she had been asked to play a part in an inoffensive comedy for the Strolling Players. A young and rather charming person was cast for the juvenile lead, and during the rehearsals in London and afterwards in Canterbury he attached himself wholly to Viola. Now Viola at this time was in the full prime of her beauty, and for five years had not once been told by Hay or any other man just how beautiful and desirable she was.

Young Leigh-Mariott was sensitive and imaginative. He had watched Hay jealously; had read into the normal cheery way in which he

treated his wife a non-appreciation of an exceptionally lovely woman that was unbelievable,
inexcusable. Having fallen violently in love
with Viola himself, he made what he took to be
Hay's callous behaviour his excuse for speaking
to Viola. But he was a good boy, honest and
inexperienced, who secretly clung to several
ideals which had not yet been discovered by his
brother officers and ragged out of him. He
continued to shadow Viola, but kept a painful
watch over his tongue.

The last night of the week came. Hay and
his wife were starting next day for Scotland for
the shooting. The boy had promised to take his
mother to Bad Ems. Heaven only knew when
he would see Viola again.

It happened that his part in the play was that
of a foolish young peer who had fallen a victim
to the charms of an impecunious young married
woman. This person was unable to meet her
bridge debts, and hoped to obtain the necessary
sum from the boy by pretending to return his
love. And then came a mildly dramatic moment
at the curtain of the second act, when, frightened
out of her life by the persistent attentions of the
man to whom she owed the money (the villain,

of course, very quiet and glossy, with a trick of hissing " By—God—you—shall "), she flung herself into the young peer's arms and claimed his help and protection.

At the rehearsals, and when the moment arrived on the other five nights, young Leigh-Mariott had caught Viola in his arms, and to the delight of his brother officers and other facetious people had awkwardly pretended to kiss her. On this last night, however, filled with desperation and sentimentality, the boy forgot that he was acting before a polite audience, and having the woman he loved in his arms, kissed her again and again with all the passion of a first love.

The curtain fell to enormous applause. The general verdict was that young Leigh-Mariott had improved out of knowledge. On the other side of the curtain young Leigh-Mariott found himself face to face with an indignant and angry woman.

Paying no heed to her indignation, the boy let loose the pent-up expressions that had been seething in his heart. He loved her, adored her, would sell his soul for her. She was the most wonderful, the most beautiful thing on God's earth, who was neglected by a selfish husband.

Viola flung the boy away. She was not angry

now at being kissed. He had done something
infinitely worse. He had called her husband
selfish. Archie—selfish !

Young Leigh-Mariott went to Bad Ems, and
eventually, with his regiment to India. He had,
no doubt, plenty of opportunities of falling in
love and kissing young married women in India,
which, no doubt, he took.

Viola went to Scotland with her husband.
" Selfish—Archie ! " she said to herself again and
again. It was monstrous, it was absurd, it was
too utterly libellous to worry about—it was true.

Yes, it was true. Archie *was* selfish. He left
her alone for hours together, day after day.
Not even for her sake could he give up any of
his games, or his preparation for his games. He
was a bachelor with a wife. But, after all, it was
not his selfishness that rankled during Viola's
lonely, unoccupied hours. Everyone was selfish
in one form or another. She would be accused
of selfishness for desiring him at her skirts the
whole day long. She did not, after this discovery, object to his selfishness. What filled her
with discontent and bitterness, anger and a sense
of injury, was the fact that, when he was with
her, he regarded her cheerfully and contentedly

as an accepted fact, an institution—a wife, and not as a woman whom he had been very lucky to marry. Young Leigh-Mariott had found her beautiful enough to lose his head and his heart. She would have been perfectly happy if Archie would sometimes make love to her as he did before they were married, if he sometimes told her that she was beautiful, that he appreciated her, that, so far as he was concerned, she was the only woman in the world.

If she had told Hay that this was how she felt, he would have stared at her in blank amazement at such childishness and burst out laughing. She knew that. She knew that Hay had no imagination. She knew that he was the sort of man who only saw just those things that were plain and on the surface, never going underneath, never looking for deeper meanings or finding other readings to a string of words than they were intended to convey.

And so Viola nursed her grievance for many months, finally taking with her to the golf cottage greater feelings of discontent and bitterness, anger and a sense of injury, than ever she had known before.

CHAPTER XI

WHEN Hay strode out of the cottage there was
a touch of delicious heat in the young May sun,
and not a tree within five hundred yards to keep
it from him. The cottage, quaintly and rather
preciously built, sat, gardenless, upon an odd
piece of land on the fringe of the downs known
as the Chantonbury Ring. High up it sat on a
miniature down of its own, and to the right and
left, in front and behind, swept the illimitable
close-cropped undulating country, rising in some
places very near to the sky and slipping down
in others to the quiet valleys, sheep-dotted,
green here and there with regular sweeping
lines of fast-growing corn, greener here and there
with rich pasture land, broken sometimes by
a belt of trees, vivid with young leaves, cut
sometimes by a white winding road which looked
like a narrow ribbon.

The air was tinged with an invigorating pinch
of salt and was alive with the gay songs of
distant larks, into which the soft minor notes of
sheep-bells joined harmoniously. Away to the
right, lying quietly in a hollow, was a small

group of red-roofed cottages. But for the sheep below moving slowly, heads down, nothing moved except on the road, along which, from time to time, a motor-car sped silently like a quick-running ant—a speck, a black spot, a larger black spot, a speck again.

As Hay started out, greatly relieved at Peg's interpretation of the position of affairs—the accuracy of which he never questioned—one phrase that had been made use of by Billy's wife rang in his head : " Make love to your wife."

This seemed to him to be a very odd and peculiar thing to say. " Why make love to Vi ? " he asked himself. " She and I are husband and wife. She knows that I love her and I know that she loves me. How can I make love to her, being her husband ? I mean, how can I make more love to her than I do by being her husband ? . . . I wonder if that's just one of Peg's bright remarks ? ' Make love to your wife.' She can't have meant it seriously. Good heavens ! she has all that I can give her. She's never grumbled. We've been perfectly happy. I grudge her nothing. She knows without my telling her how proud I am of her, that she is the only woman who has ever been in my life,

or will ever be. . . . ' Make love to your wife.'
It must have been a joke. . . . Still, as women
seem, according to Peg, to think very odd
things, I'll go and find Vi, get rid of old Billy
for a bit, and pump her. Perhaps he is hurt
with me about something, or, much more likely,
perhaps she's a bit bored here. I suppose it is
pretty dull if one doesn't golf."

By this time, all these thoughts having passed
slowly into his brain, he had come to a plateau on
top of the highest point of the country. Upon
this stood the strongly built bungalow which
served excellently well the primitive purposes of
a club-house. Its white verandah faced the
sun. Its windows were open. The whole com-
pact building beamed with cheeriness and spotless cleanliness. Half a dozen young ragamuffins
of all ages between twelve and eighteen were
playing a game of football with a tight bundle
of rags. They saw the approaching figure of
Hay and made a simultaneous rush to the professional's shed. A short, square-set, solemn-
expressioned man, deeply tanned, appeared at
the door and touched his cap to Hay, disappear-
ing instantly into the shadow of the shed, having
apparently named the boys who were to carry

for the Major and himself, for two of them raced eagerly to the front of the bungalow and the remainder of them fell into dismal attitudes.

A big man, going grey, run into immense fat, came out of the bungalow in a state of good-tempered rage. He was followed by a sullen-looking lad who carried a rug.

" But I 'ave shook it, Mr. Wright," he said.

Mr. Wright got out of his flannel jacket and rolled up his shirt-sleeves. " You 'ave, eh ? " he replied. " Then Mr. Wright's wrong."

Catching up the rug, he slapped it a dozen times against one of the verandah posts with all his might. Dust poured forth. Then he flung the rug over the lad's back.

" A good sort of shook yours, 'Arree," he said, " I don't think. There's a sack hangin' over your 'ead, my fine feller, unless you pull yourself together. The sack of Damocles and a nice dam sack to carry 'ome to father. Don't let me 'ave to do any more shookin' for you again, darlin'."

Hay came up.

" Ah, Major," said Mr. Wright. " Teachin' the young idea, y' see." He wiped the sweat from his forehead and rolled down his shirt-sleeves, smiling broadly.

" I saw," said Hay. " Fine exercise, Wright."

" For brain as well as body, sir. The duties of a club steward don't end with orderin' of victuals and drink, and seein' to it that the 'ouse is nice and sweet for members, eh ? "

" I suppose not," said Hay, looking to the right and left for some sign of his wife and Hutton.

" Puttin' something of the fear of God and Mr. Wright into these young wasters ain't included in my weekly inadequate wage, but it's done all the same."

" You seem to like it. You never look so good-tempered as when you're angry."

That was Mr. Wright's chance. He was a tender-hearted, sterling man, with the wide knowledge of humanity that is acquired by twenty years' service in the police force, from constable to divisional inspector, blessed with a temperament that was sunny in the darkest hours, and a sense of fun broad enough to relish a joke even against himself. He was also generous, thoughtful, and sympathetic, but he could not resist the temptation to point his conversation with apt quotations.

" Nature, my dear sir," he said, " hath framed

strange fellows in her time. Some that will hevermore peep through their heyes and laugh like parrots at a bagpiper; and other of sich vinegar aspect that they'll not show their teeth in way of smile, though Nestor swear the jest be laughable."

"Quite so," replied Hay, who had no notion that Wright was proudly spouting Shakespeare, and mentally labelled him, not for the first time, as an excellent but rather wordy person. He nodded and made his way round to the professional's shed.

Mr. Wright got into his coat. He was slightly damped. He had expected to win a smile or a pleasant word. As he re-entered the bungalow he reminded himself that soldiers were proverbially ill-read people, and repeated the quotation aloud word for word, in a round, rolling voice. Passing into the large, airy smoking-room, the floor of which was covered with a bilious-coloured linoleum, he bent down with difficulty to pick up a piece of fluff, and, being in that position, stroked the smooth back of a fat grey tom-kitten with a white shirt-front and four white stockings, straightened up, and made his way with a sort of swagger to a writing-table. At this he seated himself sideways, and while singing the first verse of " Come into the garden, Maud," with much expression, made various entries in his book relating to the upkeep of the club. The kitten, purring violently, sprang upon his broad shoulder, with erect tail. Wright cursed him playfully for his affection, but permitted him to remain.

" Morning, McNay," said Hay. " If it's all the same to you, I must scratch our appointment."

" Ah ? " said McNay, who was plucking a pristine Black Dot from its paper covering.

" I'm sorry."

" Ahm sorry too, sir, but it'll no inconvenience me."

Hay picked up a new iron from the rack of clubs and played an imaginary shot. " I'm looking for Sir William Hutton. Seen him this morning ? "

" No, I've no seen him yet," replied the obviously disappointed man, most of whose spare time was spent in teaching beginners, and who had been looking forward with zest to a few holes with the Major.

Hay was too keenly interested in the play of the shaft of the iron to notice the minor inflection in the little Scot's voice. It was characteristic of Hay, by no means an unsympathetic man, that he never noticed the inflection in the voices of the people who spoke to him. He heard what they said and was satisfied. When a man or woman said no he accepted it as final. He did not wonder whether, because the no sounded half-hearted or came with hesitation, he ought to say " you're quite sure ? " or " you mean that ? " Naturally enough, therefore, there were many people who habitually said no and yes when they meant yes and no to whom Hay was singularly unsympathetic. McNay found him so. Not being " in a poseetion " to say that he was " vera seek " at losing his game, he hoped that the strong touch of disappointment which he allowed his voice to contain would melt the Major's heart.

But, wholly unconscious of the professional's endeavour, Hay put the club back among its untried fellows that stood shaft to shaft along the wall, ran his eye round the shed with the ardent golfer's lust for purchase, breathed in the aroma of cobbler's wax, dubbin, sawdust, and oil, nodded, and strode out into the sun.

His duty was to find Billy Hutton and Vi.

Peg Hutton had pointed that out to him clearly. He would miss a very useful and necessary hour with McNay—which was a nuisance. And now that he felt perfectly certain that there were no reasons for jealousy, there did not seem to be any reason to give up this hour. He had started out with the intention of finding these two, however, so find them he must.

His favourite tune was listened to with annoyance not only by McNay, but by the two caddies who were waiting in front of the bungalow. As the big figure of the Major disappeared down the incline and the whistling could no longer be heard, a giggle rose from the unchosen caddies and McNay said, " Darm it."

CHAPTER XII

It was an affectation of Peg's to say that she did not like writing letters. She was never so happy as when, pen in hand, a pile of excellent writing-paper at her elbow, she sat down, all alone, to answer her numerous correspondents.

She was an admirable letter-writer. She did not content herself with dashing off a few ill-punctuated, ill-constructed lines. Hers was a pretty, clear hand, and what she wrote was written with a certain style, some wit, and evident enjoyment.

She indulged in graphic descriptions of scenery and people ; accounts of conversations, of weather, of sky effects, of social functions, of dress. She took an intelligent if purely partisan interest in politics, and often greatly amused her friends in the Cabinet, or who had been in a Cabinet, or who were in or putting up for Parliament, with a shrewd little comment, a biting criticism, or a touch of satire on the questions before the House.

There were three people to whom, however busy she might be, she made a point of writing a weekly letter. One was her father, Admiral Sir Harry Wilmot. Another was her old nurse, who had been pensioned off and lived in South Hampstead with a married daughter. Another, a young brother at Oxford, in her letter to whom she frequently folded a small cheque.

She chuckled at the remembrance of her conversation with Hay. The bare notion of any man being jealous of Billy filled her with amusement. Before commencing her letter, she dismissed the whole thing from her mind. Meakin and Stanner quietly cleared the table without disturbing her, and it was not until she had written four pages and put her hand out for a second sheet that she noticed the snivelling girl, some feet from her elbow.

" What's the matter, Stanner ? " she asked kindly.

Stanner burst into tears. " Oh, your ladyship."

Peg had taken a fancy to the girl, and tears always awakened her large fund of sympathy. " My poor child, I hope you're not in trouble ? "

" Oh, your ladyship, I d-d-don't know how to tell you."

" Dear me, I hope it isn't Meakin."

" N-no, your ladyship. Meakin has got some dreadful ideas, but he's always been a gentleman to me."

Peg had infinite patience and some curiosity. " What is it, then ? " she asked gently. " Did one of those old gipsies tell your hand and see a dark woman in your palm ? "

" N-no, your ladyship," sobbed the girl. " I only believe in tea-leaves."

" But my good girl, it's so difficult to do anything for you if you won't tell me what it is. Have you a pain anywhere ? Has your father written for money ? Is there a mouse in your bedroom ? "

" No-no, your ladyship."

" Come now," coaxed Peg, " dry your eyes and tell me all about it. You're not taking up my time. I can write my letters later."

Stanner screwed herself up to face what she conceived to be her duty. She had never been so frightened in her life.

" It's—it's about Sir William, your ladyship."

" Sir William ? " echoed Peg blankly.

" Sir William and Mrs. Hay," the girl hurried to say.

Visions of an accident floated before Peg's eyes. She rose from her chair nervously. " Well, well ? Go on."

" Oh, my lady, I'm almost afraid."

Peg caught the girl by the shoulders and shook her. " I insist on your telling me at once," she said sternly.

Stanner hesitated no longer. She rubbed her eyes and cheeks with her handkerchief and did her best to control her voice.

" It's about their carrying on, your ladyship," she said.

" Carrying on, carrying on ? I don't understand." The rustic expression conveyed nothing to her.

"Carrying *on*," repeated the girl, laying the accent on the second word. "Meakin and I couldn't help noticin', and I think it my duty to tell your ladyship, although Meakin did say that if I told you he wouldn't go on keeping company with me."

Peg's mystification deepened. At least there had been no accident. What else mattered? "Well, well?"

"I can't help it, your ladyship, but Sir William tried to kiss Mrs. Hay at breakfast and said he was crazy about her. And so he was; we could see it through the keyhole. And Meakin said he knew his way about and was a great boy."

There was a moment's silence. To Lady Hutton as well as to Stanner it was a moment into which many feelings crowded themselves. Fright, a desire to run, panic, amazement at her own temerity were some of Stanner's. Intense annoyance, apprehension, shock were some of Lady Hutton's, but annoyance predominated. No north-east wind cut more keenly than Lady Hutton's quiet voice.

"Leave the room," she said.

" Yes, my lady. But I felt it was my duty——"

" At once, if you please."

" Yes, my lady. And oh, my lady, I'm so sorry for you."

Stanner caught her ladyship's eye and hurried, sobbing, away.

For many minutes Peg remained standing where Stanner left her with her eyes blazing. " What impertinence," she thought. " To come to me with such a story, to come sobbing and talking about her duty. What impertinence. She must be sent home. She has not been sufficiently well trained. I must speak to her mother, or write. What imper——Sir William tried to kiss Mrs. Hay, and said he was crazy about her, and so he was——"

The door was flung open violently. Hay came in with rage and despair stamped upon his face.

CHAPTER XIII

" You were wrong," he cried.

Peg pulled herself together, although Hay's unusual appearance and uncharacteristic roughness added to her sense of apprehension.

" A woman who isn't wrong isn't a woman," she replied, with a brave attempt at cheerfulness. " Is anything the—the matter ? "

Hay flung his cap into a chair. " Everything's the matter. Yes, everything. And you are partly to blame."

Peg was genuinely astonished. " I ? What have I done ? "

Hay's temper was out of control almost for the first time in his life. " It isn't what you've done. It's what you've not done ! "

" Well," said Peg, in a quiet, level tone, " tell me what to do."

" It's too late for you to do anything. You've let things slide and the worst has happened. *I* must act now."

" What do you mean ? " cried Peg.

Hay started to pace the hall. " I'm trying to keep calm. But if I say anything calculated to hurt your feelings, please make allowances for me."

He took several turns silently. Peg studied his face anxiously. She had never seen Hay agitated before. She had never supposed that this studiously courteous, self-controlled, self-complacent, strong man could be agitated.

She dared not allow herself to think. She watched him blankly.

" You've all been making a fool of me," he said suddenly, as though struck by a new thought. " I'm the harmless, trusting husband who doesn't count. Well, we'll see."

" I think I have a right to ask what's happened," suggested Peg, a little timidly.

" Yes," cried Hay, " we'll see. The trusting husband isn't always so harmless as he looks. . . . I knew there was more in this affair than you said. Why you should have tried to drug me into indifference is more than I can understand. I told you they had been together day after day, hour after hour. But I've known your husband nearly all his life, and I thought that he was a man of honour. I was wrong. He's a scoundrel."

" Be careful, Archie," said Peg quietly.

" I'm sorry," said Hay. " But this is not the moment for politeness. I say that he's a scoundrel."

Peg had herself well in hand. " Why, please ? " she asked.

Hay took another turn before he spoke again. Lady Hutton's self-control was a reproach. He forced himself into a semblance of calmness.

" I hope," he said, " that what I am obliged to tell you won't hurt you as much as it hurts me. . . . When I went over to the course, having thought over what you had said, I came upon them suddenly in the coppice. I saw your husband deliberately take my wife in his arms and kiss her."

" What ? " gasped Peg.

" Curse him ! " cried Hay. " Curse him ! "

Peg was a very precious little woman, equable, sensible, broad-minded, and endowed with a keen sense of humour. But she was, for all that she possessed these angelic qualities, exceedingly and delightfully human. She faced Hay angrily, stormily.

" You call Billy a scoundrel," she cried, " but what choice word do you apply to your wife for permitting herself to be kissed ? "

" I apply no word to Viola. She's my wife."

" But I can apply a word and an equally strong one. I hold your wife entirely to blame."

" You can't."

" I do. I know Billy."

" Then why didn't you stop these incessant meetings ? "

" For that reason. He flirts, but if a woman is a nice woman he's harmless."

" You imply that Viola is not a nice woman ? "

" She allowed Billy to kiss her."

" I must ask you to withdraw that."

" I must ask you to withdraw your remarks about Billy."

" There is not a decent-minded man in England who won't call him what I called him when this ghastly affair is known."

The rally came to an end. Through all these quickly spoken sentences these two civilised people had been facing each other angrily, every inherited sense of refinement and polish having vanished under the stress of emotion and exasperation.

But Hay's last remark flung a new bomb at Peg's feet.

" Known ? " she echoed lamely. " What *do* you mean ? "

" Do you suppose," replied Hay slowly, " that I am going to continue living with Viola after this ? The affair has gone out of our hands. It must be settled in the Divorce Court."

Peg stared at Hay with an expression of horror. She saw that he meant what he said. She saw that the position was a very serious one, even more serious than she had supposed. She went over to the window and stood there for a moment, taking long breaths of the sun-warmed air.

" Good heavens ! " she said. " What are we doing—you and I ? We're losing our tempers and barking at each other at the very moment when we ought to be most friendly, most sympathetic. . . ." She came back. " Archie, I'm sorry. Forgive me."

" I beg your pardon," said Hay. " I was out of control. This is the . . . the worst thing that could have happened to me in life."

" It may be the worst thing that can happen to either of us if we meet it in this spirit. How foolish, how lacking in imagination we must be to dream of the Divorce Court as the only solution."

" What other solution can there be ? " asked Hay miserably.

" I don't know," replied Peg. " We must find one. The Divorce Court—never, never. After all, what has happened ? My husband has kissed your wife."

It certainly sounded a small matter. Among the lower classes men and women who had never seen each other before kissed each other. It was a harmless and well recognised game in which great crowds took part. At Christmas-time, among all classes, men and women kissed each other under the mistletoe.

" How can we be sure that it has not gone farther than that ? " asked Hay.

Peg had an answer. " Simply because I know Billy and you know Viola."

" But how can we tell that it will go no farther ? "

" Ah, that's the point. That's the work we've got to set ourselves to do. To see that it goes no farther."

" Viola was in his arms," said Hay. " I can see nothing but the Divorce Court for her sake."

" For *her* sake ? "

" She evidently cares more for Billy than she does for me. She had better have him."

Peg shot out a sort of laugh. " Over my dead body, dear Archie," said she.

Hay sat down. The action was eloquent. Plainly enough he owned himself beaten.

Seeing this, all the inherent pluck in Peg's nature came to the top and with it came a return of common sense. She also sat down, and putting her chin in the palm of one hand and her elbow in the palm of the other, began to think.

CHAPTER XIV

THROUGH the open windows the far-away throbbing notes of the larks came in, and the soft tinkle of sheep-bells. A gentle breeze puffed against the chintz curtains and half lifted the top leaf of the *Spectator* that lay upon the window-seat. An old grandfather clock, standing erect in one of the corners, gave forth his steady tick-tock, and a party of house-martins, hard at work with their nests upon the wall under the roof, twittered busily. The door was half open, and a maid could be heard brushing and rubbing.

Hay got up, shut the door—the place seemed alive with sounds—returned to his seat, and looked at Lady Hutton nervously and helplessly.

For the first time in his life he felt impotent, chaotic, unable to pull himself together. He felt like a man does who comes slowly back to his senses after a knock-out blow. Anger, the natural desire for revenge, the animal lust for punishing because he had been punished, had left him. His whole body was now tingling with pain. It seemed to him that the sky had lost its transparency, the downs their colour, the sun its warmth. Vi, his wife—the woman he loved and had married—Viola !—who loved him, or was supposed to have loved him—supposed !—was kissing another man !

Was kissing another man !

Peg sat curiously upright, with her hands clasped together. Her chin was tilted, and her small oval face completely without expression. Her eyes were fixed straight ahead and were wide open. There was something deliciously girlish in the lines of her figure. The sun fell in a golden patch upon the many-coloured rug at her feet.

" Who," said Peg at last, " knowing us, would have conceived it possible that we could have become melodramatic at the first touch of trouble ! Goodness knows how many happy marriages have been put into print just because people have acted melodramatically instead of with a sense of humour."

Hay looked up irritably. " I don't see how an appalling affair of this kind can be treated humorously."

" I didn't say humorously. I said with a sense of humour. Every tragedy that has ever been played can be turned into a comedy by the application of a sense of humour."

" I don't understand," said Hay humbly.

" I'm not sure that I do, quite," replied Peg, " but let's try. . . . Here are two straight and charming people making fools of themselves. One is bored to desperation, dissatisfied and unhappy. The other can't resist a pretty face. Both are married to people who love them and whom they love. If, because of the first mental aberration, they are divorced, four delightful people are to go through the rest of life wretched and miserable. Obviously the duty of the other two is to show the erring couple at once the future that awaits them. Do you follow me ? "

" Yes," said Hay. " But how ? "

" Well, anyway," said Peg, with a touch of her characteristic gaiety, " we've got half-way there. We've arrived at the how. . . . The things that we've *not* got to do are quite clear. We've not got to dare them to go any farther on pain of Divorce. To dare people not to do a thing is the best way to make them do it. . . . They must be shown, without knowing that they are being shown, precisely how foolish they look."

" I don't understand," replied Hay.

Peg sprang to her feet excitedly. " I do,"
she cried, " and I've got it. Yes, I've got it."

" Got what ? " asked Hay eagerly.

" The solution. The way to bring back our
respective better halves sorrowful and repentant."

Hay was on his feet. " I hope to God you
have," he said.

Peg went up to him and put her hand on his
arm. " You and I must pretend to do what
they are doing—only more so. Do you see ? "

" No," said Hay, " I don't."

" Try and be bright, dear man. Think hard.
You and I must caricature their behaviour so
that they will be disgusted with it. More than
that. It will drive them wild with jealousy, and
that will be simply splendid."

Hay took a step back and gazed at Peg with
wide-open eyes. For a moment he could find no
words.

" You and I—are to do—what they have
done ? " he gasped.

" Good gracious, Archie, don't be so literal.
I said pretend to do."

" Go about together all day—have meals
alone—ki-ki——"

" Kiss, yes. That's the idea. A moral lesson."

"I should hate it," said Hay. "I beg your pardon," he added hurriedly.

"Oh, don't mind me," said Peg, with a laugh.

Hay's back was very stiff. He looked almost ludicrously uncomfortable and insular.

"What are we to do first?" he asked.

Peg gave the question a moment's consideration. "Did they see you when you—saw them?"

"Yes. I—spoke."

"Oh, did you? Am I too young to hear what you said?"

"I asked them to come here as soon as possible."

"You did? Why?"

"I said that I should have something to say to them."

"Dear me, that rather complicates matters."

"Does it?" said Hay anxiously.

"No, it doesn't. It's good. It helps us. In fact, you couldn't have said anything better."

"Why?"

"I'll tell you. The thing is as clear as daylight. When they come in, put on the air of a man who is going to make a disclosure."

"Am I going to make a disclosure?" asked Hay uncomfortably.

" You are, indeed ! "

" Good Lord ! " he said.

Peg went on eagerly, excitedly, gaining most of her habitual cheeriness as her plan unfolded itself. " You are going to say, sorrowfully and yet with an air of great underlying joy, that this is a great day in the lives of us all, or words to that effect ; that you have only been waiting for a chance from Viola to show her the real state of your heart. Her conduct with Billy is the chance you have waited for."

" Good Lord ! Why ? "

" Because, you will say, it has freed you ; because you have to confess that you have grown to love another woman—me. *Moi qui vous parle.*" Peg smiled beatifically and tapped herself with a finger.

Hay made a gasping sound of horror and amazement.

" Breathless, isn't it ? " added Peg. " Then, having done with them, you will turn to me, looking as much like Childe Harold as you can. With a quiver of emotion in your voice you will then tell me that you adore me, that I am the most beautiful creature on earth—which is passably true ! And then, in a final peroration worthy of Byron, you will ask me to trust my life to you ! "

" Phew ! " said Hay.

" I'm glad it takes you like that," said Peg. " That's the effect I hope it will have on them. Now, you quite understand ? Think of all the actor-managers you have ever seen and let it rip."

Hay's hand went up to his tie. " I'll do my best," he said.

" Brave man," cried Peg. " And oh, won't I play up too ! "

" But," said Hay slowly and painfully, " suppose they really love each other, Peg."

" Then," replied Peg gravely, " in that case we shall have cleared the way for them. But, my dear Archie, they don't really love each other. They'll bluster and say they do, because they'll look such fools, but they won't break up their homes for untold gold. You see, we use up our superabundance of electricity in dozens of energetic ways. They don't, and the sun fires it—that's the trouble."

" Very well," said Hay. " It's a desperate scheme, and one that won't come easy to me to carry out. But I will do anything under heaven to win back my wife."

" Then," said Peg, " let me have your word of honour that you will not give the plan away to Viola till you've got my permission."

" On one condition."

" What's that ? "

" That you let me have yours not to give it away to Hutton till you have my permission."

" I swear." Peg held out her hand.

Hay grasped it. " I swear," he said.

Peg broke into irresistible chuckles. " So will they," she said, " when they see me stroking your hair. Sssh ! here they come."

" I hope to God that we shall succeed," said Hay fervently.

" Amen, dear friend," whispered Peg. " Now, act, act for all you're worth."

CHAPTER XV

BILLY HUTTON and Viola Hay came up from the valley in silence. Unaware of the fact that Viola had permitted him to kiss her only because she had seen Archie swinging towards them, and was determined to force the success of her desperate scheme, Billy's first sensation was one of utter disgust.

Archie was an old and dear friend of his, in whose eyes he would rather stand well than in those of any other man. He would not have cared to have been caught by him kissing anyone except his wife. To be caught—the word made him shudder—kissing Viola made him profoundly ashamed of himself. He had received his friend's order to return to the cottage without a word. He knew that he must have looked horribly foolish. He disliked looking horribly foolish almost as much as he disliked being seen when looking horribly foolish.

He walked up the hill slowly. He wondered uneasily what in the world Archie was going to say; he hoped fervently that he would have the decency to say nothing of the incident, the indiscretion, to Peg; he wished first that he had not entered into the sharing arrangement, and that, second, Viola had not been so bewilderingly pretty. He assured himself without self-deceit that his peace of mind had not been upset in the smallest degree by Viola, that his intention had been merely to pass the time pleasantly with her, and to pretend—artistically, of course, it was always good enough to do a thing well—to be desperately in love. He had passed time equally pleasantly and equally artistically many times. He owned to himself candidly that he was a man who was infinitely attracted by women. He always was more amused and interested in the society of pretty women than in the society of men. Women were necessary to him. He liked to fetch and carry, to undertake commissions, to receive letters and to write them. He liked to listen to women, to watch them. He liked charming frocks, small talk, the delicate suggestion of scent, the curve of a beautiful chin, a well-dressed head, pretty hands and nails. Just as some men found their best pleasure in picture galleries, in old curiosity shops, in fishing-tackle shops, in gun shops, in engineering shops, he found his pleasure in the society of pretty women. Women were, so to speak, his hobby, not merely because they were women, but because, being women, they were graceful and filled the eye. His was a purely platonic hobby, a purely artistic manner of amusing himself. The moment that he remembered that the particular charming woman for whom he happened to be fetching and carrying was a woman his interest in her filtered out. The moment that the impersonal element in his friendship departed he wished to bring the matter to an end.

Hay's appearance just at the precise moment, when, having kissed Viola twice, he had suddenly become bored with the episode, was more than a nuisance. Directly after having kissed Viola the second time he began to wonder what excuse he could make to her to take her back to the cottage, hand her over to his wife, and join Archie on the links.

With every step in the direction of what was certain to be a very unpleasant interview, Billy's feelings became more and more those of an injured person, a person who had a distinct grievance. It was bad form of Hay to pry upon them, to come up suddenly without giving warning—especially as it was entirely owing to his treatment of his wife that she was in the kissing mood. He deserved all he got. He should have kissed his wife infinitely more often himself. And, after all, what had he, Billy, done ? " Dash it," he repeated inwardly, again and again. " What the devil *have* I done ? I've only kissed the lady, that's all."

At any rate, he was, he told himself, not going to stand like a schoolboy before his housemaster. He was not going to stand, feebly and inanely, to receive a moral lecture. Hay would have to be very careful in what he said. If he showed temper he would get temper. If he indulged in what are called home truths he would get home truths. His attitude in the matter depended altogether on what attitude Hay took up.

Viola, on the contrary, returned with a definite and carefully prepared plan of action. So far as she was concerned, her scheme to fill her husband with jealousy, and make him alive to the fact that her beauty and magnetism were appreciated by other men, could not have worked more successfully. She was delighted with the way in which events were shaping. She looked forward to the interview eagerly. Nothing could give her greater pleasure than to find Archie furiously angry and indignant. She wanted him to demand an explanation, and then, if she was satisfied that he had really suffered, really been upset and shaken out of his complacency sufficiently well to understand the feelings that prompted her to take such drastic steps, she would make a clean breast of her grievances and kiss again with tears.

4

So Viola Hay and William Hutton passed the
golf-house, up and down and up, with the sun
falling warmly upon them, and made their
thoughtful way to the cottage. Neither had
eyes for the exquisite new greenness of the earth,
the petulant cries of lambs and the affectionate,
proud answers of their mothers. Both were well
aware that they had arrived at a crisis in their
lives, to Viola vital, to Billy humiliating and
unpleasant.

CHAPTER XVI

BILLY entered the cottage first. There was a
touch of swagger in his walk and aggression in his
manner. He felt hideously self-conscious and
uncomfortable. He stumped into the hall and
flung his cap into a chair. He saw that Archie
was standing stiffly and gravely by the side of
a settee, upon which, to his dismay and annoyance, he saw his wife.

Instantly he saw that Peg was wearing an
expression utterly foreign to her. She sat in a
curiously humble, dove-like attitude. In place
of her usual cheery, active manner was one which
struck him as disagreeably romantic, effec-

tively dramatic. Her attitude seemed to him to be irritatingly angelic. Her eyes were fixed upon the floor, her hands clasped upon her lap, her shoulders rounded. His hot temper blazed.

The rustle of a dress drifted into the room. Viola gave a curious cold little laugh and walked with her peculiar swan-like movement into the hall. She shot a quick glance at her husband and at Peg, whose presence there surprised her. She then deliberately arranged the cushion in the most comfortable chair and sat down, drumming her long fingers lightly upon its arms.

There was a long uncomfortable pause.

Unable to bear the silence and momentarily losing his self-control more and more, Billy turned his head towards Archie.

"Well," he cried. "Go on. What the devil do you mean to do about it?"

"I am genuinely sorry to be obliged to keep you waiting," Archie replied, with a touch of pedanticism which made Peg choke back a desire to laugh. "The situation is, I find, a little difficult to comprehend."

"There is not much comprehension needed," cried Billy, his hot temper making him say anything that first came into his head that he thought would annoy Hay. " I love your wife and she loves me. There's the thing in a nutshell."

All the other three gasped, Viola not less than Hay and Peg.

Hay controlled his rage with an effort. " No doubt that part seems to you easy of comprehension. I admit the narrowness of my point of view. It's the final issue that requires thought, I find."

Billy had instantly realised that he had said something diametrically opposite to his real sentiments. In his surprise and alarm he began to bluster.

" We'll go to Monte Carlo if you like," he said, " or Timbuctoo. I don't care. We'll pot at each other, if it 'ud amuse you."

Viola threw back her head and gave an affected laugh. Billy's unexpected statement carried things much further than she ever intended them to go. She tried to hedge.

" Really ? Are we in the Middle Ages ? " she remarked. " Are such things done ? In any case, is there any need for theatrical extremes ? "

Hay steadied himself. He knew that Billy always said things when his temper was hot which he greatly regretted afterwards. He devoutly hoped that this was the case now, that in his anger and humiliation he had wildly over-coloured the true state of affairs. After all, he was concerned not with Billy, but with Viola. She had not said that she loved Billy. Gripping the back of the chair, he made up his mind to carry out the prearranged plan to the best of his ability. He cleared his throat and changed his feet.

"Viola," he said quietly, "my excellent friend Billy, and my dear Peg, before we go any further, let us agree to carry through this not particularly pleasant scene without descending to melodrama. I told you, Peg, why we are met here."

"You told her?" cried Billy, with a burst of incredulous scorn.

"I told her," repeated Hay.

"Good Lord! That's your idea of friendship."

Peg feared that Hay would lose his self-control. She felt his hand shaking on the back of her chair. There was an ominous pause, but when he spoke again his voice was steady.

"We will waive the fact, Hutton, that you and I have been friends for years. We will waive the fact that Viola has been Peg's friend since school days. We will agree that all's fair in love."

He gave a little bow in the direction of Viola and Billy.

"Oh, get on, for the Lord's sake," snapped Billy, to whom Hay's manner was alarmingly puzzling.

"You tell me that you and my wife love each other. I presume that you mean for ever and ever, passionately—till death parts you?"

"You presume damn well right," said Billy.

"Very well then," continued Hay, "there is no need for us—I mean Peg and I—to consider either of you. You have looked after each other so well. Consideration must be given solely to us—Peg and me."

"Why drag in Peg? Can't you leave her out of this?"

"I am coming to that," said Hay. "The question to be settled this morning is this: What is to become of us—Peg and me? . . . Please understand that we have no intention of ending this matter in the usual way—there is something so banal about the seventh day in the Divorce Court, still proceeding. There is another way. We must follow your example— Peg and I."

Billy nearly jumped out of his skin. "What's that?" he gasped.

" What did you say ? " asked Viola, hardly knowing whether to believe her ears.

Hay ventured to glance from his wife's face to Billy's. The look of absolute amazement that he found on both encouraged him to continue.

" I said that Peg and I must follow your example. But there must be no scandal, no publicity. With you two under the same roof to satisfy the requirements of convention, Peg and I will lead our lives together."

He bent over Peg tenderly and sank his voice. Viola and Billy gazed at him wordlessly.

" Peg," he continued, " there is no longer any need for us to control our passion. I have hitherto been loyal to my wife as you have been loyal to your husband. It has been a great struggle for us both. By their disloyalty to us they have at last given us the opportunity we have longed for. My darling, will you trust your life to me ? "

With a keen sense of the drama of this extraordinary position, and more than ever determined to make Billy and Viola bitterly regret their folly, Peg did not reply at once. She allowed an artistic pause to follow Hay's appeal.

Then she got up slowly and gave her hands to Hay, catching as she did so Billy's expression of open-mouthed distress and Viola's wide-eyed horror. For yet another moment she was silent. Her simulated emotion was so painful that even Hay was moved. When at last she spoke it was in a low vibrating voice.

"I will go wherever you go," she said. "All my heart is yours."

PART II

CHAPTER I

MEAKIN led his bicycle down to the road from the cottage. He wore his characteristic indoor trousers and they were scrupulously black. Over his white shirt, however, he had put on a coat and waistcoat of brown flannel with a broad white line, the waistcoat cut with a wide opening, the coat delicately waisted and built to perfection. He had discarded his indoor shoes of a quiet black in favour of brown ones, boned and polished as only he knew how to bone and polish. Further, as his errand was to take him into the village, and the village lay some three miles

away, he wore not the discreet black bowler hat
of servitude, but a rather bold black and white
check cap, large, flat, and fashionable, with a
stiff peak. Many well-informed and psychological people very easily might have mistaken him
for an Anglican curate in semi-mufti, bent upon
healthy and invigorating exercise, such exercise
being peculiar to those parsons who are English
at heart though Roman in their observance.

So long as he was in range of the cottage,
Meakin retained the precise manner which had
been inherited by him from his Duke Street-
St. James's father and grandfather, and which
he had been proud to retain and emphasise during
the fifteen years of his gentleman's gentleman-
like career. Once out of range of the cottage—
a cottage, it was true, but a cottage patronised
by his master and his master's friends ; a golf
cottage, and no ordinary cottage—Meakin rested
his bicycle against the hedge that lined the
dusty road, brought forth a cigar, punctured its
end lovingly—it came from Sir William's favourite
box—lit it with care, mounted the bicycle with
a more jaunty and holiday-like air, and rode at
an easy pace along the middle of the road. The
psychological person would no longer have mis-

taken him for an Anglican priest, for he had not
found it in his heart to remove the red and gold
label which corseted the cigar. This little weakness proved conclusively that he was nothing
but a well-fed, well-groomed, well-shaven, very
common man.

The morning had ripened. The light breeze
from the sea which had done its best to turn over
the outer page of the *Spectator* an hour before
was barely apparent on the road beneath the
downs. It was not yet eleven o'clock. For all
that, the sun was delightfully warm. The sky,
flecked here and there with thin filmy lines of
white cloud, was blue and almost transparent.
The trees, in their first flush of youthful green,
threw motionless shadows across the white road.
The ditches on each side were alive with eager
green growth not yet made shabby by the summer
dust. Sparrows flew in regiments, with a quaint
whistling noise, from one patch to another of
the cultivated land, green with the heads and
shoulders of oats and barley. A contingent of
heavy-flying silent crows made intermittent black
patches against the sky. Parent thrushes darted
about among the hedges paying welcome visits
to their hungry and appreciative young, and but

for all these feathered, one-purposed things it seemed to Meakin that he had the world to himself.

Meakin was a Cockney by birth and inclination. All the same he was keenly alive to the sounds and business of nature. As he rode, he noted with much pleasure and with some quiet patronage the progress of the earth, the energetic and capable doings of animal life, the exquisite freshness of the colours to the right and left. He had a great respect for the bee and some little fear. He was glad to see this indefatigable little fellow about again, hard at work. As a staunch Conservative he welcomed the appearance of the primrose, and was moved to pleasant remembrances of his adolescence by the sight of the sturdy dandelion. The suspicious stinging-nettle, already head and shoulders taller than any of the other hedge weeds, he eyed as he passed with the antagonism of the man who has not forgotten a trusting boyhood.

Before he had left the second milestone very far behind, however, Meakin, whose love of human nature was far greater than his love of still nature, began to wonder why he had been hastily sent off to the village with two telegrams to dispatch. Naturally he had read them. One was to Colonel Wedderburn and the other to Alexander Maclean, and both contained apologies and regrets for being " obliged to postpone the foursome arranged for the afternoon."

These telegrams, and the note to Captain Grant-Duffie that had been hurriedly sent off to the club-house by the boy at the moment when Meakin left the cottage, set his mind working. He had seen Major Hay swing off towards the club-house directly after breakfast. He was in the middle of reading a second lecture to Stanner for her indiscretion in speaking to Lady Hutton, when the Major came stumping back with blazing eyes. He had heard the rumble of his angry voice in the hall, the silver tones of Lady Hutton's voice replying quickly. He had speculated upon the long silence and wished that it had been possible to catch something of the low, earnest conversation that had followed. With intense interest and amazement he had watched from an upper window the return of Sir William and Mrs. Hay, and had caught the loud, angry interjections of Sir William that had cut into the steady, quiet rumble of the Major's voice.

Hitherto, he had found the golf cottage almost too slow to be bearable. During the day his duties staved off the depression and boredom which had attacked him each long and soundless evening. During the day he had found the wide expanse of rolling country invigorating, and had taken some pleasure in the exquisite views that were framed by all the cottage windows; but the hours that followed after dinner, the hours that were cut to waste by his enforced presence in the kitchen trying not to listen to the small talk of the cook and Stanner, yawning over the day's paper, smoking pipe after pipe, struggling with what are called railway novels, presumably because they need not be taken out of the carriage, had got very seriously on his nerves. For these were the hours when, both down in Kent and up in London, he left off being the gentleman's gentleman and became a gentleman; when, while in town, generally in evening clothes built by Sir William's tailor, he patronised the Empire and the Alhambra, dropped into those theatres where plays which contained some attempt at intellectuality, some show of satire, or some small touch of humanity—his choice was, of course, extremely limited—filled the bill; or when, with one or other of his friends who had achieved high positions in his own profession—

one "did" the Duke of London, and another Orlando Chelsea, whose title was higher than that of any in Debrett in that he was always called by his Christian name alone—he watched famous billiard matches, boxing contests, or played bridge at his club, the United Imperial, whose premises were three rooms in the Blue Posts public-house.

In Kent his evenings were spent in the billiard-room of the "Hutton Arms," a rambling, comfortable, picturesque coaching inn, which was the feature of the High Street of the village, two miles from Billy Hutton's place. The table was not faultless, nor was the company quite up to his social form. Nevertheless, the tax-collector, the steward of the golf club, the station-master, the postmaster, Mr. Winchester the chemist, Mr. Parry the family butcher, who owned many acres of the land thereabouts, Mr. Hitchcock the corn chandler, whose son was the well-known trainer at Newmarket and the pride of the place, being quite the little gentleman with his yellow gloves and white bowler, his rolled cuffs and waisted coats, his long cigarette-holder and diamond ring ; and Mr. Sam Wragby, by whom was the "Hutton Arms," were all very respectable and cheerful persons. They all had their special cues, and some of them played billiards. He had introduced bridge to these persons much to the horror of the Nonconformist minister of the place, who had not taken the trouble to discover that bridge is only a modern variant of the old respectable whist, a game of which he greatly enjoyed.

To Meakin, therefore, the upset at the golf cottage came as a most welcome relief. It was plain enough to him that the Major had seen something that made him both jealous and angry. He hoped with all his heart that the arrangement for sharing the cottage would come to an abrupt termination, and that Sir William and Lady Hutton would either behave like Christians and well-bred people and return to London for the rest of the season or go to Paris. He pined for bridge, billiards, and civilisation.

More cheerful than he had been for many days, he covered the remainder of the third mile quickly. He arrived in the village imbued with optimism, and dismounted at the post-office, which was before everything else a sweetshop. This, a grocer's, a butcher's, a luncheon and tea rest for cyclists, and three inns, which were scattered about among a line of cottages, made up the village. Having handed in the telegrams with a request that they might be sent off at once, Meakin walked his bicycle to the " Cat and Fiddle " by E. Bulstrode, leaned his machine against the horse-trough, and made his way into the glasses-only department.

There was no one behind the bar, but several cheerful sounds of life came from the back premises. A child was crying lustily, a dog was barking, and hens were celebrating the arrival of their eggs.

Meakin tapped on the counter with half-a-crown. Mr. Bulstrode made his appearance in his shirt-sleeves. He was the pale type of man, whose face and hands freckled abundantly.

" Good morning, sir," he said.

Meakin waved his hand. " Let me have a bottle of Bass, will you ? " he asked. " Child teething ? "

Mr. Bulstrode smiled. " No, sir ; broken a window. His mother is teachin' 'im." The cork came out easily and the bottle rang the glass.

" Join me ? " said Meakin.

" Oh, thank you, sir. I don't mind if I do."

The other cork came out, the two men performed the usual rites and drank.

Meakin glanced round the primitive room, with its bare floor, wooden benches, and coloured advertisements of whiskies, indulgently. Now that there seemed to be a chance of getting away from the place its rusticity suddenly became amusing. He remained in the " Cat and Fiddle " for an hour. During this time he accounted for another bottle of Bass and a second cigar, and at Mr. Bulstrode's earnest request he examined the list of horses which were running in the races of the day and passed judgment upon them. He dazed the rural innkeeper with his expert knowledge and inside information. With the confidence and assurance of all inveterate backers away from the race-course he divided up the probable starters into three classes—the not outs, the no earthlies, and the best things in racing. With the cunning of all prophets, he took care to give at least three horses for every race as the certainty, and for his star nap plumped at once for a horse called Socrates, for another horse called The Imp, and for a third animal cryptically named Outsider.

When Meakin left the room and went out again

into the sun Mr. Bulstrode anxiously reviewed the position. He found that Socrates was bound to win if it rained, that The Imp couldn't be stopped if the wind was in the south, and that Outsider would walk home if he liked his jockey. So E. Bulstrode made up his mind to have a shilling on each of these horses to win. He sat down to make a list of the horses he had been told to put his shirt on in the other events, and got so utterly and hopelessly mixed with the not outs, no earthlies, and best things in racing that several of the races were run before his list was complete. Whereupon he backed nothing, and had the satisfaction of being able to tell his customers in the evening that he had lost a considerable amount of shillings that day without being a penny out of pocket.

When about a mile from home Meakin's quick eye caught sight of three familiar figures. Their attitudes were so uncharacteristic that he nearly fell off his bicycle. Going slowly up the downs were the Major and Lady Hutton. Her ladyship was clinging to the tall man and resting her cheek against his arm. It was the attitude of an amorous housemaid. Some distance behind them, stalking like a Red Indian, Meakin saw Sir

William. Whereupon, filled with excitement and wonder, he gripped the handle-bars, rounded his shoulders, and made for the golf cottage at the top of his speed through the mid-day sun.

CHAPTER II

OUTSIDE the cottage strong moonlight silvered everything. The wide expanse of sky had a very pageant of stars. The breeze had fallen. Not a sound broke the melodious stillness of the evening, the beautiful peacefulness of Nature's few sleeping hours.

Inside the hall, in the evening of what had been the most eventful and amazing day in the lives of the Hays and the Huttons, there was an air of peace and homeliness.

A large lamp on a thick pillar of silver burned warmly, throwing a soft yellow light upon the pitch-pine walls that were stained a dark oak tint, upon the many charming prints that hung upon them, upon the polished floor covered here and there with skins, and upon the oak furniture fashioned curiously but with an eye to comfort.

The air of peace and homeliness was contradicted by the facial expressions of Meakin and

Stanner. The man, who was peeping out of the
window from behind the curtains, had the
appearance of a cunning and mischievous smooth-
haired terrier. His eyes were twinkling excitedly
and a half-smile played round the corners of his
mouth.

Whimpering foolishly and giving an occasional sob—the outcome of excitement rather
than of grief—Stanner was clearing away the
last signs of dinner.

With a quick, expert movement Meakin darted
away from the window and caught up a handful
of dessert knives and forks. His expression was
that of a domestic who takes a keen personal
interest in his work.

Sir William Hutton came in. His heels rang
on the floor.

" Pack my things," he said brusquely.

Not a sign of the intense surprise caused by
this unexpected order showed itself upon the
well-trained face of the valet.

" To-night, Sir William ? "

" At once. Then carry my dressing-case into
the village and order me a bed at the best inn.
I return to London to-morrow early."

This was exactly what Meakin most desired.

" Shall Stanner pack for her ladyship, Sir William ? "

" No. . . . Don't stand gapin' at me. Carry out your orders."

" Very good, Sir William."

Hutton lit a cigarette and threw it away, bent down and flicked the dust from his stockings, and kicked the leg of an unoffending chair.

" Where's Mrs. Hay ? "

" Mrs. Hay left the dinner-table, Sir William, to doctor the spaniel."

" Did Mrs. Hay dine alone ? "

" Oh dear no, Sir William. Madam dined with her ladyship and the Major."

" Good God ! "

Hutton's involuntary exclamation contained nothing of blasphemy, but it was big with amazement and disgust. He swung round on his heels and went out into the night.

Never in his life had this man, who had grown accustomed to being treated by Providence as though he were the spoilt boy of the human family, to whom no great sorrow had ever been meted out, who always had enjoyed splendid health and a substantial banking account, who never had been punished for any of his small indiscretions, and who knew just how to fall on his feet as though he had been trained for acrobatics, been so completely upset, confused, nonplussed, outraged, alarmed, shocked.

The amazing and horrible declaration made by Hay, and the eager acceptance of it by his wife, seemed to Billy Hutton to be the most unEnglish, the most artistically frightful moral *débâcle* of which it was possible to conceive. That the man whom he had known as intimately as though he were a brother—more intimately than many men know their brothers because Hay had been his closest friend—since he was a young boy, and the woman with whom almost every day of five years had been spent, should both suddenly show sides to their characters as to the existence of which he had never dreamed seemed to Hutton to be treachery.

He assured himself that if he lived to a hundred he would never get over the awful shock that they had given him. For the first time in his life he was brought up sharply face to face with trouble. He stumbled out of the cottage as soon as Peg slipped so eagerly and pathetically into Hay's arms, and wandered blindly about repeating over and over again, " My God. I've

lost Peg. She doesn't love me. She never loved
me. I may as well die."

So new a thing was suffering to Hutton that
although he said these things to himself with great
despair and emotion, it was some hours before
he realised actually the horror of the situation.
At first the whole thing seemed a sort of night-
mare, something which might affect Viola, his
wife, and Hay, but which could not affect him.
He was like a child who is told that his little
brother is dead, and that he will never see him
again, and immediately goes upstairs to find
him to play bricks with. He had read of
tragedies, had been moved to surreptitious tears
at the representation of grief upon the stage,
but had never come face to face either with
tragedy or one of the few incidents that renders
life intolerable for the time. He was lucky enough
to have lost neither of his parents, nor any of his
brothers and sisters, nor a friend. Pain, mental
and physical, were strangers. He was obliged to
go over the whole scene again, and then again,
before he was able to realise its full significance.
And when, at last, he did realise it he demanded
of Heaven some reason why of all men he should
be selected for punishment so frightful.

He told himself that he would be lost without Peg. He tried to think what he had done to give her cause to cease loving him. He tried to find something in Hay that could possibly be more attractive to her than all his own undoubted attributes. He tried to think of the moment when Peg had ceased to love him. He threw his mind back over the years and months, went wildly back over all the days that he could remember, recalling her words to him, her expressions, her looks.

He absolutely refused to accept any blame for what had happened. He had done nothing, nothing at any time, that could be put forward to excuse Peg's desertion, Peg's deceit, Peg's treachery. He came to the conclusion that both Hay and his wife had hidden from everyone some dreadful characteristic. All the same, this conclusion did not soften his suffering. If anything it heightened it, because it hit his vanity. He had considered that he had known both of them so well.

Without being aware of it, he walked quickly, trying to keep pace with the rush of thoughts. For the first time since his childhood he was so overwhelmed that he was unable to think of any of his small moment-by-moment self-indulgences. He forgot that such things as cigarettes and cigars existed. He forgot that he was uncomfortably hot in a rather thick suit of Skye tweed golf clothes. He was wholly occupied with the pain that was caused by the martyr's wreath of thorns.

Finally he found himself two miles away from the cottage, down in the valley in the bottom of which the village lay. He sat down on the stump of a tree on the edge of a copse. To the right and left of him the earth was alive with primroses, with celandines, and with forget-me-nots. Everywhere Spring's children were at play, delighting in an exquisite sense of life. The copse, made up for the most part of young, sturdy trees, with here and there one of middle age, and with one or two old and gnarled fellows that had braved innumerable winters, not without the loss of limbs, wore their greenest and freshest colours. A thousand throats throbbed with song. Bees hummed, and insects kept up an incessant undercurrent of orchestration. But only one voice rang in the ear of Billy Hutton, and that was his own. " I have lost Peg," he repeated again and again. " I have lost Peg."

He had spent an hour arguing himself out of this appalling conclusion. He had succeeded only in proving his conclusion to be the right one. He had lost Peg. He had lost her not from any fault of his own. He was blameless. He had nothing with which to reproach himself. He almost wished that he had. He had lost her solely because she loved another man. It made him very bitter to think that he had really lost her some time before the knowledge had been brought home to him. It was unthinkable.

With his eyes on the green carpet at his feet, patterned with delicate colours, he called up a host of scenes in which his figure occupied the centre place, in which he was the tragic hero. He saw himself passing through life alone, smileless, except when it was necessary to persuade curious friends that he was unhurt. He saw himself, still alone, gradually growing old, childless, unloved, with a home that was the husk of a home, uninterested in all his old pursuits, unattracted by those things that attracted him most, a wanderer, a passer-by.

Never before, now that Peg was no longer his, did he feel the need of her so poignantly. It never had occurred to him hitherto, for the simple reason that he had never been obliged to give a thought to such a matter, that Peg was so completely part of his happiness. He felt like a steamship engineless with no land in sight.

This simile pleased him so much that he repeated it to himself several times. Other nautical expressions came into his head. He was derelict, rudderless, the horizon showed no hope. He regarded himself with intensest pity and commiseration. And then he looked up.

Utterly unaware of his presence, he saw his wife and Hay. She was hanging on his arm with her face upturned. About her lips a smile of ineffable happiness played. Her slim, sweet figure seemed to be moving unconsciously. The sight of happiness so exquisite brought him back to the present with a crash. He no longer felt like a hero, an insubstantial creature standing about in attitudes of correct misery and Christian-like mildness. Rage and jealousy seized him by the throat. Nothing would have given him greater pleasure than to have rushed forward, seized his wife by the shoulders, and shaken her so that her beatific smile might have been chased away by a look of pain. His one desire was to fall upon his treacherous friend and spend his rage in blows.

The lovers passed on. They made a beautiful picture.

She might have been Undine and he Huldbrand, Knight of Ringstetten.

For some time Hutton made no movement. Then, shaking with anger and despair, he dogged their footsteps at a distance. He was like a man who, having received a wound, rubs in salt.

CHAPTER III

AND what of Viola? Exactly how hard did this unexpected blow hit her?

Viola was one of those women whose powers of reasoning, dormant during ordinary times, are set in motion by the unexpected. At first, the sight of the man who had won all of her heart, whom she loved fiercely, hungrily, with another woman in his arms, filled her with a mixture of anger and anguish. It was a sight utterly unbearable. It was a sight that could not be borne with feelings kept under control. She rose quickly, sped to her room, locked herself in, flung herself face down upon her bed, and gave way to an agony of tears.

The first thing that stared her in the face was

the blankness of her future life. Like Hutton, she told herself that life was at an end. She would live, she supposed, and walk and eat and dress, but she would not be alive.

Like Billy Hutton, and not unlike all other men and most women, she instantly became the one interesting and beautiful figure in a long series of cinematographic pathetic pictures. She had had her grievances before the explosion of this bomb. She was right in supposing that they were genuine grievances. She was the neglected wife up to an hour before. Now she had become the deserted wife, the woman with the broken heart. All her hopes lay shattered. Her little plan, undignified though it might have been, somewhat humiliating as it certainly was, had been conceived and carried out for good and not for bad. If it had been successful Archie would eventually have been thankful to her for her deceit. If it had failed no harm would have been done, either to herself, to Archie, to Billy Hutton, or to his wife. Of the four she would have been the only one to have paid something of a price for its conception. She would have damaged her sense of dignity. As it was, it was only too successful in a way the bare idea of which never had for one moment crossed her mind. Her desire had been to stir Archie out of his complacency. She had done so. She had, by appearing to be attracted to Billy, given Archie the excuse that he needed to declare his love for another woman.

When Viola, her beautiful face wet with scalding tears, her carefully dressed hair not unbecomingly dishevelled by contact with pillows, arrived at this point of her conclusions, she sat up suddenly with a jerk. An expression of reviving intelligence flashed over her face. A look of eager hope came into her eyes.

She rose from her bed. She began to walk up and down the narrow, dainty room. At first her walk was slow. She seemed to be feeling her way. Then unconsciously her pace quickened. Her brain was working so quickly upon a new and wonderful line of thought that to have kept pace with it she wanted to run. For some little time her lips remained compressed, her eyes narrow, her hands clasped in front of her. Then, again suddenly, she drew up, and threw up one long hand with its fingers distended. If she had been a man she would have cried out, "By Jove!" As it was, being very much of a woman, she said, " Ah ! . . . Ah ! " and began—she who only fifteen minutes before had been torn with grief—to laugh, quietly and triumphantly.

And then she sat down at her dressing-table and commenced expertly to remove all traces of tears.

Now Viola was a clever woman, an observant woman, and a woman of spirit. She had not passed the greater part of her life among men and women of the world for nothing. Not wholly unconsciously she had studied character and temperament. She knew pretty well what men and women did under given circumstances. Only pretty well, because no one knows, especially the man inexcusably young who stands firmly upon his hind legs and says, after having read a book or watched a play, that such and such a thing is improbable and could not have happened, exactly what men and women, civilised and uncivilised, are capable of doing. Everything can happen, and nothing is improbable. The improbable is precisely that which one does not happen to have seen. Viola did not happen to have seen any previous signs of this great passionate love so flagrantly and shamelessly confessed to by Archie and Peg. Therefore—it was improbable.

Starting with that faint speck of light at the other end of what had seemed to be a tunnel without an end, Viola began to think. Step by step, always with her eyes fixed on her faint white speck, she made her way up through all the years of her married life. She re-examined Archie's character and temperament with the utmost care. She confirmed her preconceived ideas of both. A man deeply imbued with an honesty so golden, a simplicity so limpid, a definition of right and wrong so insular and so, if you will, arrogant, could not have carried on an illicit love affair without obvious unrest of mind. If, after marrying one woman, he had fallen in love with another, either he would have forced himself immediately out of love with her or made a clean and dignified breast of it to his wife. That, at any rate, would have been like the Archie Viola thought that she knew. If, however, her knowledge of him was imperfect, was only superficial by reason of her love for him, at any rate it was not so hopelessly at fault that she would not have been able long since to have seen that he was hiding something from her and everyone else.

She introduced Peg to her husband again—

Peg, her oldest friend, the cheery, charming, beautiful Peg, already engaged to be married to Archie's closest friend. She examined all their subsequent meetings in London, in the country, abroad. She passed through again their holidays together at Montreux, at Cairo, at Monte Carlo, in Scotland, Ireland, Skye, and Newfoundland. She revisited country houses under whose roofs all four of them had stayed for the hunting, shooting and fishing, cricket and golf. She went back to South Africa with Peg, where, during the Boer War, they had acted as nurses while their husbands were in the fighting line, Archie with his regiment, Hutton with his yeomanry. She went back to the restful period when, the war over, they spent the whole of one summer together at one or other of their houses, trying to forget the hardships and horrors that still were all too vividly fresh in their mind.

Step by step, the faint white speck becoming whiter and larger, she brought herself through the last winter, when they all hunted in Leicestershire, through the beginning of the season, when they dined and theatred together almost daily, to the very cottage one of whose

5

bedrooms she was pacing, more and more quickly.

And then she cried, " No, no ! They don't love each other. They never loved each other. They never will love each other. They are pretending to do so. . . . Why ? "

She laughed. It was so obvious, so childish, so amateurish. No, not childish and amateurish, because she herself had been pretending to be in love with Billy. Without knowing it, they were imitating her. Thinking, and being horrified to think that she was seriously in love with Billy —after all, Archie had seen them kissing, after all, they had been inseparable for eight days— they had adopted her very plan in order to win back Billy and herself.

It was too funny, but it was also too satisfactory for words. It proved beyond the shadow of a doubt that she had won. It proved conclusively that Archie had been becoming uneasy, and had finally, upon discovering Billy and herself in a lover-like embrace, become tragic. It also proved how tragic he must have become to have fallen in with a plan that was obviously invented by Peg. Archie was incapable of invention.

Her laughter rippled out as she imagined how disagreeable and irksome such pretence must be to such a man as Archie. Naturally enough, her respect for him deepened—now that she was mistress of the situation—because of the admirable way in which he had carried through a difficult scene. She never would have given him credit for such excellent histrionic ability. Of course Peg acted as well as she did everything else.

And then Viola noticed how brightly the sun was shining, what a superb panorama was framed by her window, how delicious was the gentle breeze.

For some time she sat smiling before her glass, applying cooling creams to her cheeks and removing these with a nicely perfumed astringent lotion. Then she changed her dress.

CHAPTER·IV

" THEN," said Meakin when Sir William Hutton was well out of earshot, "we do not connive, we do not condone, and neither are we in collusion. All the same, my child, it is what is vulgarly known as thick."

" I don't know what you mean," said Stanner, rolling up the napkins.

Meakin's face relaxed into a smile. " Sir William Hutton plucks Mrs. Hay from the Major's garden, and the Major lifts Lady Hutton out of Sir William's glasshouse. Whereupon Sir William becomes moral and clears out, and I see myself in the witness-box of the Divorce Court in a red tie and a fancy waistcoat."

" It's awful."

Meakin eased his collar with a long forefinger. " Ah ! " he said, " wait till you've been a bit longer with the best people."

" I believe you enjoy it all," whimpered the girl, " that I do."

" Next to playing in a billiard tournament," replied Meakin, with real enthusiasm, " there's nothing I like better than watching the aristocracy at play."

" S'pose someone takes me away from you when we're married. What'd you say then ? "

" I should alter his features so that he wouldn't be recognised by the family circle. But, you see, dear, it's different in our case. We can't take out Debrett's special licence to play ducks and drakes with the commandments."

There was a short silence in the half-whispered conversation. The girl, very pretty and prim, moved silently from the table to the dresser. With a slight air of condescension the man, who did not wish Stanner to forget that he was kindly lending a hand—pigging it, he called it—moved the chairs away and lifted the table back against the wall.

" Oh, poor Sir William," said Stanner.

" It's poor Sir William now, is it ? It was all poor Lady Hutton this morning."

" That was before she took up with the Major. I think it's disgraceful."

Meakin stiffened. " My good girl," he said severely, seeing his opportunity for some fine talking, " you mustn't utter those sentiments in an atmosphere of lions rampong on cushions argong."

Stanner would have been impressed if she had not been so agitated. " What are you going to do ? " she asked.

" Stick to Sir William, of course. It won't take long to get used to a new lady."

Stanner placed the lighted candles on the mantelboard. " I shall leave her ladyship," she said. " What sort of a name shall I get in my village if I stay on with a new master ? "

" If it gets as far as your village, my dear child, you'll be doing your father a good turn to stay on."

" How, Jimmy ? "

Meakin gave a slight shudder at the plebeian shortening of his Christian name, but was not to be diverted from saying what he considered to be a really bright thing. " Why ? " he said, " he'll become a popular figure through you and get all his drinks for nothing."

Stanner gazed at her hero with wide reproachful eyes. " Only fancy looking at this dreadful business like that ! "

Meakin placed a tin of cigarettes near the lamp. " There are two ways of treating life," he said sententiously. " The practical, which is making life do what suits *you*, and the damn silly, which is letting life do what suits it. Take these things into the kitchen."

Stanner took the tray of finger-bowls. " Aren't you coming ? "

" In a minute or two. I just want to get up to date with the state of the game."

He went quietly to the window, peered out, and fell back in a convulsion of suppressed laughter.

" What's the matter now ? " asked Stanner nervously.

Meakin coughed and drank some water. He put his mouth close to the girl's ear. " The Major and her ladyship are coming towards the cottage, and Sir William is watching them from the coal-shed like a recording angel. What a subject for the coloured supplement of a Christmas number ! "

" It's a very wicked world," said Stanner.

" It 'ud be a dreadfully dull place if it wasn't," replied Meakin.

The girl left the hall. Every line of her figure showed how scandalised she was with the philosophy of the man who had won her rustic love and admiration.

Meakin was on the point of following her when the rustle of a gown and the ripple of a charming laugh pulled him up.

Lady Hutton entered the little hall, bringing, it seemed, something of the silver moonlight with her. If anything she looked more cheery and bright, and more light-hearted than usual.

" Has Sir William come back, Meakin ? " she asked.

" He has, my lady."

Peg glanced at the table. "But you've cleared! Has Sir William dined?"

"I think not, my lady, unless Sir William partook of pot-luck in the village."

Peg unwound a gauzy white thing that was wrapped round her head, and which gave her a stronger resemblance than ever to Romney's Lady Hamilton.

"Where is Mrs. Hay?"

Meakin's manner disclosed nothing of the intense interest he took in the peculiar situation. "Mrs. Hay is putting another bandage on the spaniel's leg, my lady."

"I see," said Peg. "And Sir William is upstairs?"

"No, my lady, Sir William is meditating in the coal-shed."

Peg turned away quickly. An almost irresistible desire to laugh seized her. Her voice was unrecognisable when she spoke again. "Thank you, Meakin," she managed to say.

"Thank you, my lady," returned Meakin. Whereupon, being dismissed, he disappeared, gently and disinterestedly.

Once alone and unobserved Peg danced to the window. "Archie!" she called. "Archie!"

A ringing voice answered.

" Come in, quickly."

Hay's step came lightly and swiftly. When he entered his face no longer had upon it the stamp of misery and unhappiness that was there in the morning, nor the artificial passion that he had struggled to wear during the epoch-making interview. He wore a boyish, eager smile.

" Well," asked Peg excitedly.

" Upon my soul," he replied in the same manner, " we seem to have done well, jolly well."

" I think so. Billy never let us out of his sight all day, except during dinner."

" And now he's in the mood to wreck the cottage."

" Where do you think he is at this moment ? "

" I dunno," said Hay.

" In the coal-shed, making up for Othello." Peg subsided into a settee and laughed and laughed.

Hay laughed too for a moment. The notion of the immaculate Billy Hutton standing on or near lumps of coal appealed even to his small sense of the ridiculous. " Yes," he said, " it is funny in a sort of way ; but—but what does it all mean—exactly ? "

Peg finished laughing comfortably, wiped her eyes with a diminutive scrap of cambric, and sat up with an air of quiet confidence and triumph.

"It means, my dear Archie," she replied, "that you are to be spared the unpleasantness of making further love to me, that instead of our having to call each other dearest and darling for the remainder of the evening we can behave like rational beings again, and above all, that you will not be obliged to spend several hours locked into my room to-night as far away from me as the walls will permit."

Hay gasped. "Do you mean to say that I should have had to do *that*, Peg?"

"That was my trump card," she replied, "in case we had failed to-day."

"You're sure that we have not failed then?"

Peg spread out her dress. "We have won the rubber with a hundred aces to add."

"It's almost too good to be true," said Hay. "I—I wonder if you're right. Don't think me thick-headed," he added apologetically. "You see, I'm a soldier, and I've never gone in for using my brains much."

"Naturally; but isn't it perfectly plain to you that Billy is rampant with jealousy?

There's not a man half so virtuous on earth as Billy to-night."

" I see that. Yes, I see that. But——"

" But what, dear Archie ? "

" But what about Viola ? "

" Well," replied Peg, with a smile, " Viola can't possibly burn her fingers in a fire that's gone out, can she ? "

" No," he replied. " No." He heaved out a great sigh of relief, tilted up the lid of the tin box, took a cigarette, lit it, and sent out a stream of smoke through his nostrils. " No," he said again.

" And so congratulations, Archie," said Peg. " The episode is over hundreds of miles away from the Law Courts."

For a moment or two Hay smoked silently. Then he marched up to Peg's settee and stood in front of her—a fine figure of a man.

" How am I to thank you, my friend ? " he asked.

Peg tilted her head and gave the matter her best consideration. Her face was serious, but there was a twinkle in her eyes. " By taking care, dear man," she said, " that you don't allow such a thing to occur again."

Hay's eyebrows almost met with amazement. " I ? . . . I ? . . ."

" Didn't I say you ? " she asked sweetly.

" Yes, but—how do you mean ? "

Peg met his astonished eyes frankly. " Haven't you been thinking just a little during the day, although you are, if you will permit me to remind you, a soldier ? "

" Yes, of course I have."

" Well then it can't occur again, can it, because, of course, as you have been thinking you have naturally seen the error of your ways and will hurry to turn over a new leaf."

Hay threw his ash into a silver tray with a gesture that had something of impatience in it. " You're joking," he said.

Peg laughed softly. " I never was more serious in my life, Archie."

Throwing away the cigarette, Hay produced his pipe, strode over to the table, put his hand into a big Doulton bowl and loaded up with an excellent full-bodied smoking mixture. " Turn over a new leaf. The error of my ways." The phrases echoed in his head. He lit the pipe, drew a chair forward, sat down, and threw one long leg over the other.

" Do you imply," he asked severely, " that *I* am to blame for this affair ? "

" I do, O man," said Peg, utterly unafraid.

" Why, please ? "

" Smoke a little more," she laughed.

Hay looked just a little annoyed. " I took this cottage with Bill. I may have been slightly to blame for that. But I trusted him, and I thought that no wife could be happier or more contented than Vi."

Up went both Peg's practical little hands. " Oh, you dear old unimaginative normal creature," she cried. " You sportsman, you honest Englishman ! "

Archie grunted and shifted his shoulders uneasily. " I don't know whether you mean to flatter me or reproach me," he said.

Peg made herself more comfortable. She lifted a cushion out of a chair and put it behind her to catch the small of her back. Then she fished a pouffe nearer and placed both feet upon it.

" Now tell me," she said. " Didn't you have a very enjoyable life before you married Vi ? "

" Of course. Why not ? "

" You fished, shot, hunted, played golf and cricket, eh ? Were an all-round crack, I take it ? "

" I don't know about that. Did pretty well, I suppose. Did my best to put in a good time, anyway."

" I see. And all you wanted to complete the perfection of your bliss was . . ."

" Well ? "

" A beautiful wife."

Archie looked unexpectedly sentimental. " Yes, and I got her, by Jove."

" Ah, what a beautiful girl Vi was, wasn't she ? Do you remember ? "

" Remember ? " cried Hay enthusiastically. " She was, and is, the most beautiful woman in England."

" And the most popular too, for four years— in fact, until you married her. I never shall forget how extremely fond of her Cecil Lambart and Kenneth Amory were, and a dozen more. . . . What a charming and exciting life hers was before she married you. A perfect hack for the Row in the morning. . . ."

Hay threw in a remark. " She could have that now if she liked."

" Ranelagh, Hurlingham, Ascot, Cowes, balls, dinners, motor runs, triumphant week-ends in all the most delightful country houses. . . ."

" But, my dear Peg, she *lives* in the country most of the time now."

" The men always at her feet, her smile something to be fought for, her lightest wish—caprice even—obeyed as though it were an order. Always the same excitement when dressing for dinner, knowing that the men were waiting eagerly to see her, and bursting to tell her how perfect, how lovely a thing she was. Ah yes, her life was very satisfactory then, wasn't it ? "

Hay did not see that Peg was running him into a trap. All the same, he resented the slight emphasis placed by her on the word " then."

" I dare say she thought so," he said, " but Vi is far too sensible to feel the need of constant compliments, constant admiration. She married me, don't you see, and settled down."

" I see," said Peg. She settled herself, henwise, among her cushions and examined her beautiful nails interestedly. . . . " You still hunt, of course ? "

" Well, you know I do. Three days a week all the season."

" And when you come in delightfully tired, Vi, in a perfectly exquisite tea-gown, gives you . . ."

" Tea, Peg, tea. I make a point of it. Never

settle down to a nap in front of the fire or rush off to a hot bath. I sit and chat to Vi, and give her full details of the run, and she . . ."

" Gives you tea. I see. Then dinner. A cheery crowd dining ? "

Hay was still characteristically unsuspicious. " Not on hunting days," he replied. " One get's so jolly sleepy, don't you see."

" Of course," said Peg, with well-simulated sympathy. " And so after dinner you and your pipe fall asleep in that lovely comfy chair of yours."

" That's the idea. Ripping chair, isn't it ? "

" Ripping," said Peg. " And . . . Viola ? "

" Oh," replied Archie, " she's a great reader, you know."

" Yes, yes, of course. A great reader, like Aunt Martha, who never had a husband. . . . When hounds don't meet . . ."

" Oh, well, then one golfs, of course, or shoots. There's lots to do."

" You and Viola together ? "

" Oh no, these things bore Vi. And I hate her getting wet. Besides, she always has a lot to see to."

" Oh, to be sure ! How stupid of me. In

the morning there are the orders to be given to cook for your meals."

" Hang it ! Her meals too ! "

" She has the stores and the linen to give out, a list of complaints to make to the servants, because you've made them to her. . . ."

" Somebody must complain ! "

" To call on stuffy country people and be at home when they return her calls, and perform the endless necessary duties of the perfect wife, while you are playing games, doing things, enjoying exactly the same glorious life that you led before you had a wife to consider."

" But, good Lord," cried Hay, now on his defence, " I don't only consider myself ! I'm always thinking of Vi."

Peg shot out a little laugh. " So tenderly and so sympathetically, dear Archie, that you leave her alone day after day, year after year, with the women who bore you stiff, the women you call deadly dull, hysterical, neurotic, fanciful, discontented."

" I don't," said Hay, " but many of 'em are. You don't imply that I've ever called Vi any of those things, do you ? " He glared at her.

" No ; but that's what you've made her, my friend."

" What ! "

" My dear Archie, look things in the face. Square your shoulders and look honestly at what the papers call the marriage problem."

Archie rose and knocked out his pipe with unnecessary noise. " I don't call marriage a problem," he said stiffly.

" Perhaps you don't. But it is a problem, for all that." Peg leaned forward eagerly, now warming to her work. " What's the trouble with women, with Viola ? A natural healthy excitement that makes the blood race through the veins and carries away the megrims is just as necessary to women as to men. After marriage you men forget that. You take care that you get your exercise and excitement, and equal care that your wife doesn't. Relaxation does she want ? Nonsense. There are all the duties of her house, of her position."

" But what more can any woman have than Vi has ? What more does she *want* ? "

" Your companionship, Archie ; your constant companionship, with at least ten per cent. of the excitement and attention and admiration that

she used to get. There is no 'used to' about
your life. You still hunt, race, golf, shoot, fish,
and play cricket. But Vi must be domestic,
eternally domestic—alone, eternally alone, with
the little petty worries, the little mean troubles
that drop like water on a stone, until she is
goaded into discontent, and from discontent into
indiscretions, until, bitter and disappointed, she
joins the women who taboo domesticity, who
hunt and race men—expensive pastimes which
cost the husband nothing because the other men
pay—the women who are driven elsewhere for
the necessary terms of endearment and flattery
which they no longer get from their husband."

"Good God!" cried Hay. "What are you
saying? *You* don't want this life?"

Peg's advocacy of Viola and all the other wives
who were suffering from her complaint had
brought a warm glow into her face. She felt,
however, just a little self-conscious for having
let herself go strongly.

"My dear Archie," she said more quietly,
"Billy is a different type of husband. He never
sees me without glorifying me out of all relation
to myself. Although I've got the sense of
humour to recognise that, I have the vanity to be

warmed and satisfied by it. You think that
Viola is too sensible to need admiration. That's
where you're wrong. Every human being needs
admiration in some form or another. We are all
egotists. We are all human beings. A man
must make love to his wife all his life, otherwise
another man will do it for him. The only possible
way to prevent hysteria, discontent, and deceit
developing in a woman is for the husband to give
her his admiration, sympathy, and a few of his
hours."

CHAPTER V

THERE followed a long silence.

For what seemed to Peg to be fully five minutes,
Hay stood gazing at her, as though turned to stone.
Then he walked slowly away, went over to the
window, and looked out upon the silver night.

Never before had he been so startled. He felt
as though he had been driving a car in the dark
at an easy regulation average speed, and had
skidded suddenly, turned a half-circle, and found
himself facing not the road upon which he had
known himself to be, but another leading in a
diametrically opposite direction. He also felt
sore and for a moment or two bitterly annoyed.

He had been found fault with. He, a man who always did everything well to which he set his hand, had been found fault with—and by a woman. A very good little woman, an uncommonly charming and beautiful woman, but a woman. To be found fault with at all was a new and extraordinary experience. Always during his life he had been praised, applauded, lionised. He did not, of course, because of this imagine that he was flawless. He had never given such a matter a thought. He was just Archibald Hay, Archibald Claude Moncrief Hay, late of the 3rd Dragoon Guards, who had been—if it comes to that—one of the youngest majors in the service, who had won the D.S.O. in South Africa for distinguished services in the field, a man who played for his county, for the I Z., who had held the All England Championship for racquets two years running. Oh, what was the good of making an inventory of all his so-called achievements. The fact remained that he was Hay and couldn't help it. And a woman had taken it upon herself not only to criticise, but to condemn his conduct towards his wife.

Hay remained at the window without a movement. Outwardly he was just as calm, and

apparently as contented as usual. Inwardly his
mind was in a chaos of contradictory thoughts.
Whether he and Peg had put a stop to what
could not be called anything but a dangerous
flirtation or not, the fact remained that Viola
and Billy had, for the time being, forgotten
themselves so far as to kiss. Why? He knew
Billy well. It never hitherto had been any of
Archie's business how often or how dangerously
he chose to flirt. But when Viola took it into
her head to behave like an amorous housemaid
it was very much his business. Was it possible
that he had driven her into such conduct? Did
he leave her too much alone? Was he con-
tinuing to lead the life he had led as a bachelor
and by his sublime, unconscious selfishness
sowing the seeds in Viola of discontent, hysteria,
perhaps unfaithfulness?

He concentrated all these thoughts on one
question. Had he left Viola entirely and completely out of his day's arrangements? . . . .
Yes, he had. Thoughtlessly, but entirely and
completely. He loved her, yet never had considered her. She was wholly necessary to his
life, yet he had never taken her wholly into it.
He could honestly assure himself that it had

not occurred and would never have occurred to
him that Viola wished to enter more closely into
his daily life. She did not care for putting herself to any exertion, she had no liking and no
knack for playing any games except bridge,
and that he only mildly tolerated. How was it
possible for her therefore to enter into his daily
life ? He never had supposed that he was expected to give up a certain number of hours
every day for the purpose of holding her hand,
or in sitting about with her and entering into
enthusiastic discussions as to whether she looked
better and younger in this or that dress, this or
that hat. He knew what he liked to see her in,
but he did not know why. To him she looked
just as well in everything that had nothing
outré about it. Neither had he ever supposed
that Viola wished him to be different from what
he was, what he was born to be and brought up
to be. But now that he was obliged to inquire
into it he was bound to confess not only that he
knew nothing whatever of a woman's nature,
but that he never had wanted to know anything. He had fallen in love with Viola's beauty,
had fallen under the spell of her personality.
How could he be expected to examine her

character, diagnose her nature, make deep psychological studies of her temperament? He was only a man, not a professor, a clairvoyant, a palmist, a doctor, or a novelist.

He told himself these things impatiently, trying, naturally enough, to make out as good a case for himself as he could. Nevertheless, it was obvious that his *laisser-faire* method with Viola was the wrong one. The result was disastrous, and might even be the means, however successful Peg's plan might be for the moment, of causing permanent estrangement. Such a thing was too painful to contemplate or allow. He agreed, humbly, that it was his duty to make concessions. He could see the fairness of Peg's arguments in favour of the wife who felt lonely. He agreed with her, too, as to the reasons of Viola's temporary and desperate lapse, because, if there was one thing that was absolutely impossible to concede, it was that she could flirt in such a way in a normal condition of mind. Yes, he would turn over a new leaf. He would begin a new chapter of his married life, and would make a point of remembering that women were different from men; that they were, in fact, very peculiar and extraordinary creatures. Viola was very peculiar and extraordinary, but Heaven knew how well worth studying and keeping happy.

And then he left the window and went back to Peg's side. There was a note of deep emotion in his voice when he spoke.

" Thank you," he said.

Peg put her hand on his arm impulsively. It was a charming sympathetic and grateful gesture in which there was nothing of triumph.

" It's not too late to make a change ? " he asked.

" Dear old boy, it's never too late. You'll be very happy again, you and Vi. Happier than you've ever been. We may all be glad that this thing has happened."

" Please God you're right," said Hay. " What's that ? "

Peg had caught the sound too. Her face broke into a smile. " Billy sneezing," she replied. " If he comes in be very kind to him, poor old boy. The victors can afford to be kind." She rose.

" Where are you going ? "

" To my room. This veil has made my hair untidy. And I want you and Billy to be friends again. Be your nicest."

" Of course I will," said Hay. " Poor old Billy."

CHAPTER VI

POOR old Billy, extremely sick of himself and all the world, had been walking round and round the cottage. Through the windows he had seen Hay and his wife, looking more lovely and desirable than ever, in the hall. He had seen a light in Viola's room and had waited for her to come down. She didn't seem to be coming down. So, feeling extremely homesick and weary, Billy made up his mind that Hay should not keep him out of the hall any longer. Hang it, they were still sharing the cottage. He had an equal right to the hall at present.

He walked in slowly and sulkily, went over to the tobacco table and took a cigar.

Meakin entered, with candles for the card table.

Hay took up an insular position with his back to the fireplace. Inwardly he was just as uncomfortable as Billy was outwardly. He thought of a dozen cheery things to say. None of these came easily.

" First-rate weather," he said finally.

Hutton pretended that the remark was intended for Meakin. Meakin knew that it was not. Neither replied.

"The days are lengthening splendidly," added Hay.

Billy shifted his shoulders and struck a match violently. It broke. He swore under his breath.

"In to-day's paper," continued Hay pluckily, "I see that there are more rumours of a general election."

Billy broke another match.

Meakin watched the little comedy with keen delight. To hear one man talking to another whom he had known pretty nearly all his life as though he were a club acquaintance struck him as being irresistibly funny. He had the greatest difficulty in preserving his gravity. He lingered about the hall, doing wholly unnecessary things as silently as possible.

Hay continued to make small talk.

"There's not a bad article by that man Hutchinson on golf to-day. It's true that most of his column is given up to shoe-nails and the right way to spell putt, but at the end he says one or two decent things about the length of clubs. Have you read it?"

Billy broke a third match. He swore aloud.

" Meakin," said Hay quietly, " give Sir William a light."

Meakin picked up a lighted candle, went to Hutton, and held it out towards him.

" Go to blazes," said Billy between his teeth.

Meakin bowed.

Quickly and quietly Hay made a movement towards the servant, took the candle from his hand, placed its flame within a foot of Billy's nose, and waited.

He waited twenty seconds. During this time Billy, irritated and annoyed, and not sure that he was not making a bit of an ass of himself, hesitated, looked at the candle, at the cigar, at Archie, at the candle again, and finally accepted the hospitality of its flame.

" Thanks," he said.

Hay caught Meakin's eye and nodded towards the door. The man reluctantly obeyed the silent order, and left the room in the unsatisfied frame of mind of the person who is obliged to leave a theatre in the middle of an interesting act. Hay found that he had not succeeded in breaking the ice. Billy sat down stiffly, picked up a magazine, turned over its pages petulantly, and smoked in a gusty way.

Hay tried again.

" It don't seem to me," he said, " that those golf articles can do a man any good. Why does the ordinary player want to know how to kill worms or thicken the greens ? And as the information is got from the green men they naturally don't want it. Bad padding, these things, I fancy. Don't you think so ? "

" Dessay," muttered Billy.

A long-forgotten picture returned suddenly to Hay's mind's eye. He saw a round-faced boy in white flannels sitting in a lonely corner of the school pavilion. A pair of gloves had been flung down upon the floor and a bat heaved on to a pile of clothing. It was W. B. C. Hutton, rising twelve, who was sulking because A. C. M. Hay, skipper of the second eleven, had put him in first. He disliked going in first. It always meant his being dismissed in the second over.

If Hay had not spent eighteen years in the Service and fallen under its deadening influence of self-conscious etiquette, he would have gone over to his old friend, given him a mighty punch of affection and put an end to the scene. As it was he remained in his erect correct attitude and cleared his throat.

" Been round to-day ? " he asked.

The question drew Billy at last. He twisted round and glared. " You don't suppose," he said, very slowly and with much emphasis, " that I've been able to play golf to-day, do you ? "

" Why not ? "

" Most fellers wouldn't have had to ask me that."

Hay puzzled over the cryptic remark for a moment or two, failed to find in it anything of sense, and dismissed it.

Billy flung his cigar away. He was too down-hearted to enjoy tobacco, and too dispirited to treat Hay to the volley of reproaches that his disgraceful conduct deserved.

Hay was quite incapable of understanding Billy's mood. This was as well. If he had known that he was looked upon by his friend as a wrecker of homes there would have been high words. So Hay continued to regard Billy as bad-tempered and Billy to regard Hay as callous.

Hay took out his cigar case. " Try one of these," he said.

" No, thanks."

An uncomfortable silence followed.

Archie had done his best to be his nicest. He

couldn't do more. He went over to a corner of
the hall, took up a putter and putted imaginary
balls into an imaginary hole, with the infinite
painstaking calculation of the genuine golfer.

This time it was Billy who spoke. " I should
think," he said sarcastically, " that you're pretty
tired."

" Why ? "

" Well, you've covered a goodish bit of country
since breakfast."

Hay detested lying, but Peg had not given him
permission to withdraw from their position.
" We didn't see you," he replied lamely.

Billy scoffed. " That was very obvious."
The sight of the man who had ruined his married
life playing unconcernedly with a putter was
too much for his temper. It began to boil.

" Yes, we did a good many miles. It's a really
delightful place."

" Oh, devilish delightful ! "

" I'm surprised it isn't better known."

" The morals of the place will be notorious
enough presently, thanks to you."

Hay drew up suddenly. " To me ? "

" Yes," snapped Billy loudly, " to you."

Hay controlled his desire to take Billy by the

shoulders and shake him till his teeth chattered.
As it was he marched down upon him quietly.

" Look here," he said. " I'm doing my best
not to rake up anything unpleasant. " I'm perfectly ready to let bygones be bygones. But if
you're going to say things like that . . ."

Billy sprang to his feet and faced up Hay.
His eyes were blazing. " Well . . . Go on."

Viola saved the situation. She sailed in in a
charming dress that fitted like a glove. She saw
both men, but looked only at Billy. Her face
brightened. She went towards him with a well-
simulated air of girlishness.

" Oh, there you are ! " she cried. " I've been
looking for you everywhere. Where *have* you
been ? " She caught him by the lapels of his
coat, in a proprietary manner.

" Don't," murmured Billy.

Hay gave a laugh. " Billy has been prospect-
ing for coal," he said.

" Oh ! " Viola's tone was polite, and she regarded her husband with wide eyes and slightly
raised eyebrows, as though he were a mere
member of a house-party whom she had never
met before. " What exactly does he mean ? "
she asked of Billy.

" Oh, that's wit, y'know," replied Billy through his teeth.

" I'm sorry, old chap. It was a heavy joke."

" Twenty-eight shillings a ton," said Billy.

Viola's expression was immensely well done. " I don't follow these innuendoes," she said.

" They weren't innuendoes," said Billy. " They were Rickett Smith's."

Hay burst out laughing.

" What on earth are you laughing at ? "

Hay smiled and stood widely on his legs. " I think we know, don't we, Vi ? "

He received another cold indifferent look.

" Do we ? " asked Vi. She sat down.

Hay instantly sat down on one of the arms of her chair. " Why, of course we do. All's well that ends well, eh ? " He said this in a tender whisper, bending down towards her. He endeavoured to convey to her not only his humble apologies, but the fact that he intended to treat her very differently in the future.

Viola got up. She wore the air of a woman who disliked anything like familiarity on the part of a person about whom she knew nothing and wished to know nothing. She went to Billy.

6

"You must be awfully hungry, dear?" she said lovingly.

"I had some food in the village," replied Billy.

"Oh, my sweet old boy! Why didn't you come in to dinner? I hope you're not going to make me worry about you at the very beginning."

"The very beginning of what?" asked Hay, hurt, amazed, and angry.

Viola assumed an expression of bashful nervousness. She almost giggled. It was horribly clever. "I—I can't very well say in front of a—a third person."

"A third person!" gasped Hay involuntarily.

"Look here, drop this rot, Vi. Billy, I believe your wife would like to see you. She's up in her room."

"Is she? Did she say she'd like to see me?"

"She didn't say so. But I know that she would."

Billy turned eagerly towards the door.

Viola laid a restraining hand upon his arm. "I have first claim on you now, dear William," she said gently. "You must bear in mind also that it would not be quite in the best taste for you to see Archie's wife in her own room."

Both men cried "*What!*" together.

" I know," Viola continued evenly. " It does sound odd ; we've none of us got used to the new arrangement yet, have we ? "

That was too much for Hay. He could stand no more. He turned sharply on his heels and left the hall.

CHAPTER VII

With a triumphant smile Viola watched her husband go. Everything that he had done and said in that short interview confirmed her reading of the situation. He and Peg were pretending !

" And now," she said to the astounded Billy, " we can talk. We have got much to discuss, you and I. You've wasted one whole day— utterly frittered it away. Sit down and listen."

She put her hand on his arm again.

" Oh, for the Lord's sake," cried Billy, agitated and frightened, " don't paw me about, Vi."

Viola began to laugh. Not at Billy, not at his particularly insolent remark, but at the whole thing generally. " Yes, now I know," she said, " now I know. Oh, won't Peg be angry when she hears how foolishly Archie gave himself and her away."

" He's callous," cried Billy, " utterly callous.

Why, do you know that he actually had the audacity to pal up to me just now ? "

" Why not ? "

" Do you—do you ask that seriously ? The man who's broken the sacred bonds of friendship by takin' away my wife ? . . . You've lost the sense of decency."

" It would be an all too obvious *tu quoque* to say what you've lost, Billy."

But Billy was fairly started. He had been silent all day, chewing the cud of bitterness.

" I've known that man all my life, pretty nearly. I've punched his head, shared the same tuck basket, taken a birchin' off the same birch, made love to the same girl, borrowed his money —in fact, I've—I've been a brother to him. I trusted him implicitly. I thought he was white. That he should go back on me like this shatters my belief in loyalty and honour. I trusted him to such an extent that not only did I share a cottage with him, but left him all alone with my wife for days together while I did my level best to amuse his. There's no doubt about it. The man I've been such a true friend to all these years is a wrong 'un."

For a moment it seemed to Viola that Billy

was not talking seriously. His peroration descended from the sublime to the ridiculous and mounted to the sublime again. She put him under a searching examination. She was almost immediately satisfied that he was sincere. Although she had known him all her married life she had not seen him under the stress of emotion.

" You're speaking of my husband," she said.

" Poor old Vi, I'm sorry for you. I never was so sorry for anyone as I am for you—except for Peg, poor little Peg."

" You needn't be sorry for Peg."

" Not sorry for Peg? Lured into the power of a man like Archie ? "

" Oh, bosh ! She thinks that she's being extremely clever."

Billy was shocked. " Viola, Viola," he said, " don't go on like this. I know that you're really suffering tortures, but don't try to hide it under such appallin' callousness."

Viola leaned back upon the cushion that Peg had used. " Quite on the contrary," she replied. " The present state of affairs suits me exactly."

" Good Lord," said Billy, " you're gettin' lightheaded. You don't know what you're sayin'."

" I tell you that the way things are 'shaping

themselves is exactly how I would have them
shape themselves. It's delightful."

Billy sat down. "Well, upon my soul ! This
sharin' business is givin' me an insight into
character that I never dreamed of. You call
the—the abduction of a man's wife from under
his very nose delightful ? You call blatant immorality delightful ? "

"There has been and will be no immorality."

"But," urged Billy, "I've watched 'em larkin'
about all day like a housemaid and a postman."

Viola could not refrain from a touch of scorn.

"You are what is called a man of the world,"
she said, "and you can't see that your wife has
put Archie up to it all."

"How dare you say such a thing about my
wife."

"I tell you," said Viola, "that Peg has planned
all this with Archie to make us feel foolish."

Billy was up again. He paced the room
quickly. "Make *us* feel foolish ? What have
we done ? Good Lord, I only kissed you. If
a man can't kiss the wife of his best friend, who
can he kiss ? . . . Look here, it's no use your
shuttin' your eyes to facts. This is no put-up
game. There's no pretence about this. Those

two unfortunate people have run off the rails. I followed them for miles to-day, and the way they were romping would have done credit to Epping Forest."

Billy's buoyant and exuberant method of expressing himself even when extremely upset made Viola laugh.

" Well," added Billy, " if you're not the most extraordinary woman I ever met. I always thought that you loved Archie."

" So I do. And that's the sole reason why I made you kiss me when I knew that he could see."

Billy came to a pause. " I beg your pardon. Did you say ' made me kiss you ' ? "

" Yes," said Viola, " I did. Oh, you're a very fascinating person, Billy, but I didn't lead you on to kiss me to give me pleasure, but to give Archie pain."

" I—I don't understand," said Billy feebly.

" I know you don't. I didn't think that it was necessary for you to do so. But since you've very nearly spoilt everything by taking their ridiculous antics seriously, I am obliged to take you into my confidence."

Billy returned to his chair. He sat down heavily. He looked more boyish than usual.

" Dash me if I know what you're talkin' about,"
he said.

It had become necessary for Viola to do something to which she had a great dislike—to show
her true feelings. She rose, walked to the
window, drew in a deep breath of the clean,
pungent air, and spoke with her back towards
the man who would eventually be certain to
call himself her victim.

" I may be vain," she said, " I may be an
hysterical fool, but before we came here I was
just sick to death of everything. I married Archie
because he loved me madly, and because I loved
him. But I didn't dream that only a few years
after we were married he would treat me like a
domestic cat, and stroke me when I mewed, and
put me outside the door when he wanted peace.
He has developed into a sort of married bachelor.
All *his* pleasures and hobbies must be enjoyed,
but I must be content to slip into middle age with
a darning-needle in my hand. Never ! Never !
Never ! . . . It was no use complaining and
asking him to let me share his life. He sent for
the doctor and secretly asked him to give me
a tonic. What had to be done was to show him
how valuable I really am to him by letting him

apparently lose me, by letting him see that another man could appreciate what he had grown accustomed to. I determined to make Archie suffer, yes suffer, for all that he had made me endure. You came, and I made you flirt with me, I used you to make Archie jealous."

Billy drew in his breath. "How perfectly disgraceful," he said.

"And," said Viola, facing him determinedly, "I have not done with you yet."

"What!" cried Billy, almost comic in his agitation. "You're not satisfied with the awful havoc you've made already? You're not content with having driven my wife into the arms of another man?"

"Satisfied?" Viola's voice rang through the little picturesque room like a bell. "I've not yet begun."

"Good Lord," said Billy, "what will become of us all? You're—you're dangerous."

The beautiful, Juno-like woman moved slowly back to the settee. Well on the right side of thirty, in exquisite health, not yet in the prime of her life, she did not suggest anything of weakness or meekness.

"Every woman is dangerous whose husband

neglects her," she said. " I tell you that I have only just begun. Archie was jealous and horrified this morning. He must be made more jealous and more horrified if I am to succeed. His talk about divorce this morning made Peg suggest this pretending plan. It's plain enough to me, although you refuse to see it. And all the good that I brought about is rendered useless because you were taken in. Of course they think there is no longer any need to be afraid, because they've seen you crawling abjectly about. Can't you see that ? "

With a suggestion of excitement about him Billy got up, left the hall, and went out into the moonlight.

With a smile of impatience and of indulgence Viola made herself comfortable on the settee, and listened to his quick steps as they passed and repassed the window.

CHAPTER VIII

VIOLA had no difficulty in guessing what was passing through Billy Hutton's mind—relief and speculation. Relief at the soundness of her deduction, and speculation as to how best he might make up for his agitation, emotion, and stupidity.

Billy was one of those men who always had amused her mildly, but never had interested her very much. Two of her brothers belonged to the same type—the quick-tempered, good-looking, rather plump, good-natured, lazy, kind-hearted, blustering, pleasant, vain, unintellectual type. Knowing them, she knew Billy. She knew that he was capable of great rebounds, that deep depression was invariably followed by the highest spirits. She knew also that having shown himself to be hopelessly at fault, he would not be happy until he found many ingenious reasons to prove that in reality he was right.

So she put a curb upon her impatience and gave him ten minutes. She herself was certain that she had every reason to be satisfied with the state of affairs. But for Peg's intervention and Billy's loss of nerve she and Archie might have had a mutual clearing up. As it was, it was necessary to regain her position, refrighten Archie, and make it by her treatment of Billy impossible for him to believe that there was no need for further anxiety.

Billy came back well within the ten minutes. He had recovered his confidence.   He swaggered and rose on his toes as he walked.

" Vi," he said, " is your brain quick enough to see what the very dickens of a dance we can lead those two simple souls now ? "

Viola didn't allow herself to smile. " Is yours ? " she asked quietly.

" Oh, Vi, Vi," he continued enthusiastically, " what a chance we've got now to show them the whole art of flirtation ! I'm sorry for you, by Jove I am. I can see what a life yours is with dear old Archie. But I'll wake him up for you. What do you say ? The end justifies the means, and I'll let him see as plainly as you like how a beautiful fanciful woman ought to be made love to—you sweet thing."

He caught up one of her hands and kissed it.

" Thank you," said Viola. " That's quite good."

" May I do as much of that as I like ? "

" Certainly.   It's just what I want."

" Ah ha ! " cried Billy.

" But . . ."

Billy was performing an excited *pas seul*. He stopped.   " Did you say but ? " he asked.

" But only in front of Archie and Peg."

Billy made a little grimace. " Peg," he echoed doubtfully. " Why Peg ? She idealises me. I should hate to disillusion her."

" Because," replied Viola, with a slight distension of nostrils, " this affair has developed into a duel between me and Peg."

" Why, what has Peg got to do with you and Archie ? "

Viola laughed softly. " She understands the management of men, my good William, and she is advising Archie on the management of me."

The hall rang suddenly with a loud guffaw. " Peg understands the management of men ? My trusting, adorable Peg ? Oh ho, I never heard anything so funny in my life. Any fool knows that I am the master of my house."

" Any fool may. The fact remains that *she* put Archie up to their quite well-acted scheme, and congratulated him upon its success directly they were told that you were in the coal-shed."

" You all make an immense amount of fuss about the coal-shed," muttered Billy. " I simply stood there for a moment to get out of the moon."

Viola stood up. Her manner became practical. " Never mind about that," she said. " What I want you to do if you really mean to help me——"

"I know, I know, my dear child. You leave it to me. I can see great possibilities for pullin' Archie's leg now and havin' some fun with Peg. She's just a bit too cocksure about me, what?"

There came a laugh from the staircase. Billy seized a cushion, dropped it on the floor, placed Viola gently into the settee, sat at her feet and leaned picturesquely against her knees.

Peg found him in this sentimental attitude. She received a slight shock. All the same her voice was bright and very friendly.

"That's right, Billy," she said. "Take a rest. You must be tired after your exercise."

Billy tilted his chin. "Ah," he drawled, "it was a frightful mistake my followin' you. I thought you were Vi, y' see."

Peg darted a quick look at Viola. She found that one of her slim hands was resting on Billy's shoulder. It was the attitude of the proprietor. She also found that Viola's smile was dreamy and very peaceful, and without the least suggestion of guile. What had happened? What was the meaning of this rapid change in Billy?

"Well, the evening's young," she said lightly. "Suppose we have a rubber."

"I dunno," said Billy. "I'm a bit busy."

"We may as well, dear," put in Viola softly.

"If *you* wish it, right." Billy looked up into her face. "Can I play like this?"

"Why not," said Peg. "She'll get a splendid view of your hand."

Billy giggled. "She can hold it if she will."

"You silly old thing," purred Viola.

A slight shudder ran over Peg. She had heard newly engaged people, very young newly engaged people, say those things.

"Where's Archie?" she asked. "I left him here. We must have a fourth. I'm sorry to disturb you, Billy, but suppose you go and find him."

"Oh, blow!" said Billy.

"Run along, dear," said Viola.

Billy got up. "You've only to raise your finger, and I'll obey you like a dog."

It was the first time in their lives that these two women—school friends, old and affectionate friends, who had confided to each other nearly all their little worries and troubles, ideas and aspirations—had felt uneasy when alone. It was the first time that both felt nervous of the other, nervous and antagonistic.

Viola had said that there was to be a duel

between herself and Peg Hutton. It was quite natural then for her to look stiff and feel uncomfortable. But Peg had not yet been able to make up her mind as to what had brought about the unexpected attitude of Billy. She and Archie had seemed to have succeeded so admirably. Whatever had taken place since Billy had returned obviously must have been brought about by Viola.

Peg was more than nervous. She was frightened. Viola had acted her part so artistically, with such exquisite truth to life, she had simpered and been sheepish, had gushed and been sentimental, had, as Peg told herself, been so completely idiotic, that it did not occur to her, for a moment, that she was not really in love with Billy. This being the case, it would be easy for a woman so beautiful and so alluring to twist such a susceptible man as Billy round her little finger. It was only too evident that this was what she had done.

Peg made up her mind quickly. There was still a chance of saving the position. She realised what Viola had realised, that the future happiness of the four people in the golf cottage was to be won, not by the two men, but by the two

women, that more than ever the fight was round
Billy. He had been captured by her in the
morning, Peg thought, and recaptured by Viola
in the evening.

Peg had watched her husband leave the hall.
She then sat on the settee with Viola and smiled
at her. It was her business to be quite peaceful
and undisturbed. She found it difficult to know
what to say.

" A very affectionate old thing, Billy, isn't
he ? " she began.

" Very," said Viola enthusiastically, " so
different from Archie ! Oh ! I'm so sorry I said
that."

" Why ? "

" Why, because the Archie type attracts you,
and you naturally dislike my running him down.
. . . Isn't it convenient ? "

For a moment Peg was wordless. Viola's
artlessness took her breath away. " Have you
seen anything of Archie since dinner ? " she asked,
having nothing better to say.

" Too much," replied Viola, with a little pout.
" We found it difficult to get rid of him. He
behaved most oddly."

" Oddly ? How ? "

"I mean oddly under the circumstances. It was most diplomatic and wise of him to be hail fellow well met with Billy; there is no reason why they shouldn't be just as friendly as ever; but I really couldn't put up with the familiar manner he adopted towards me. Will you, like a dear, give him a quiet hint?"

Inwardly Peg bristled. Outwardly no woman could have been more sympathetic.

"Of course I will, Vi," she said. "But honestly, I don't think he meant to be familiar. Really, I think that the manner you objected to was the outcome of a suggestion of mine."

"Oh, what was that?" Viola showed great interest.

Peg sailed on. "Well, you see, thinking that he might find it a little difficult to know exactly what attitude to adopt towards you and Billy, I advised him to treat you in a brotherly way."

Viola's eyes narrowed. "Oh, what a good idea," she said warmly. "But what *has* become of Billy?"

"You are anxious to get to bridge?"

"No, I'm anxious to get to Billy."

"Oh, I'm so sorry that I sent him after Archie. I'll go and find them both."

They got up together.

"No, no, please don't bother. Billy would rather I went."

Before Peg could say anything more Viola had left the hall and was calling, "Billy, Billy," at the foot of the stairs.

Peg sat down again. "Good heavens!" she said aloud.

CHAPTER IX

ARCHIE heard the involuntary exclamation. "You've seen them!" he said.

"I should think I have," replied Peg dryly.

Archie threw up his hands. It was the first time that anyone ever had seen him give way to anything so un-English as a gesture.

"And we were congratulating ourselves that it was all over! . . . I never saw anything like the way in which Viola is behaving."

"Oh," exclaimed Peg eagerly. "How did it strike you?"

"I can only think that she's madly in love with him. She's driving me wild."

"I wish I could think that that's what she's setting out to do."

"She'll succeed if she goes on like this. I

can't stand it. I simply can't stand it. She's—
she's treating Billy as she ought to be treating
me ! "

" And Billy is treating her as he ought to be
treating me," said Peg.

Hay made an angry movement towards the
door.

Peg caught hold of his arm. " Now, now,
Archie," she said soothingly. " Nothing rash.
No scenes."

" Scenes ! " cried Hay. " There must be
scenes. I'm out of control."

" Then get into it again, quickly. More than
ever now you and I must keep cool. I own to
being—if I must say it—frightened. Yes, Archie,
frightened. Viola's open delight at the arrangement made by us baffles me. At this moment
I feel like a theoriser standing among the ruins
of her pet ideas. I don't know what to think
of it all."

" It's no use blinking at facts," said Hay a
little wildly. " Viola loves Billy."

" If she doesn't, her attitude is superbly—and
utterly—surprising. But the point that upsets
me most is Billy's attitude. Archie, I have never
seen him so—so sammified before."

" He's so much in love that he was actually shy in front of me."

" He wasn't shy in front of me ! " said Peg, with a rueful laugh.

Hay ground his teeth. " There's nothing to be done to save the situation. It's hopeless. Even you must believe that now."

If Hay had not challenged Peg she would have agreed with him. As it was, his definite statement, the little word " must," acted upon her as a tonic. It put her on her mettle again. It stirred all her fighting instincts and awoke the reasoning powers that had been shocked into a comatose condition by Viola and Billy.

" No," she said quietly. " I do not believe that. You're going to ask me why. It's trembling under your moustache. I'll tell you. I can still see Billy following us. That's why. His change of tactics is too sudden. Viola has been talking to him. One of these days I shall find out what she said. At present we can only make a guess. To my mind, whether she is in love with him or not, Billy is not in love with her. She has persuaded him to help her in carrying out some scheme of her own, and has proved to him in some way or another that you

and I are not serious. That accounts for the
return of his self-confidence and cheerfulness.
Are you following me ? "

Hay had been listening eagerly. Not so much
because he saw her points as that he was inspired
by her belief in them, he was becoming less
desperately despondent as he listened and
watched. Her animation, her sparrow-like alert-
ness, her absolute refusal to own herself beaten,
her conviction, carried him with her whichever
way she went.

" Yes," he said. " Go on."

Peg smiled. It was good to feel that Hay
was with her. It gave her greater confidence.
Up to this point she really had only been feeling
her way.

" There is not much more to be said, Archie,"
she continued, laying a firm hand on his arm.
" We must go on. We must carry out our
scheme to the bitter end. We won this morning
and reduced Billy to a state of abject misery.
This evening we must go much further and win
again—this time permanently. Our fight is for
Billy. Once we have convinced him that Viola
is wrong in supposing that you and I are pretending in order to make them ashamed of their

flirtation—well, if I know Billy, and, good gracious! who can know him better than I?—all will be well. He will never want to speak to Viola again until I have forgiven him. And without Billy how can Viola flirt?"

"If she loves him," said Hay, "she won't let him go."

"If she loves him," replied Peg, with her chin held high, "she will have to win him from me, and I'm a born fighter. We've yet to prove that she does. We will prove it once for all to-night. Now, Archie, no half-measures. You must not merely appear to be in love with me. You must *be* in love with me. You must whisper and sigh and glow like a harvest moon. You must gaze at me as though I were a tobacconist's girl and you a crammer's pup. I will be your Francesca if you will be my Paolo."

Hay shuddered.

Peg shuddered too. "I am talking facetiously to hide my nervousness," she said. "No more jumping at conclusions. No more mutual congratulations on a victory before the battle is over. And now listen, I have a most horribly brilliant idea."

Hay gazed at her silently. He was afraid to put the question for which he waited.

So Peg was obliged to expound in cold blood. " First," she said, " we have to behave like a pair of love-sick creatures who have no fear of ridicule and no sense of reserve. Take no notice of Viola and Billy, however greatly they may anger you. Remember that I am the only woman you have ever really loved, and that I dote on you " ; she paused, and gathered herself together. " Our one object in life now being to fill Billy and Viola with horror and amazement, we wind up the evening with a *coup de théâtre*—we say good-night and go up to my room together, and if that don't do it nothing will."

Hay groaned.

CHAPTER X

BILLY and Viola came back to the hall together hand-in-hand. Billy, now in the highest spirits, was in his most mischievous mood. No undergraduate on the night of the fifth of November was out for enjoyment with half the gusto.

Viola, certain that she was winning all along the line, was not without a feeling of enjoyment. Underlying the seriousness of events that had followed on each other's heels with such rapidity in this exciting and, she hoped, important day,

there was an element of farcicality that appealed
to her sense of the ridiculous. She was acting,
she knew that the others were acting, she knew
that the others didn't know that she knew that
they were acting, and she knew that they didn't
know that she was acting. At least, she thought
that she knew !

They found Hay and Lady Hutton sweet-
hearting, after the manner of the seaside girl
and the youth who doesn't cram for the Army
Qualifying Examination, and is passed in although the Examiners have agreed that he is
illiterate.

Lady Hutton's attitude upon the settee was
altogether charming. She was leaning back
against two large blue cushions, and her head
was tilted so that she might look up into Archie's
face. Hay stood behind the settee, and utter
devotion was stamped on his face.

Billy was intensely amused with the things
that they were saying.

" You love me with an A because I'm . . ."

" Artful," murmured Hay.

" What ! " cried Peg.

" I'm sorry. I mean artless."

" I should think so." She took one of his

hands and held it against her cheek. " And you love me with a B because I'm . . ."

" The best woman in the world."

Peg pouted, although she smiled. " You ought to have said the most beautiful."

" That goes without saying," replied Hay gravely.

" And you love me with a C because . . ."

" Because you're contented with me."

" Ah, yes, indeed ! How true, dearest, and with a D because . . ."

" Damn," said Hay, looking up as though he had only just noticed the entrance of the others.

" Ditto," laughed Peg.

Billy shot a wink at Viola and went to the cigarette table, rising more than usual on the balls of his feet.

" Now, y' know," he said airily, " this is goin' to be doocid awkward, what ? "

Viola followed him. " What is, dear ? " she asked.

" Why, this cottage."

" I've thought so all day," said Peg pleasantly. " So has Archie."

" Really ? Why ? " Viola spoke very sweetly, with her head on one side.

Peg noted with real admiration how very

beautiful and graceful her friend looked, and how very much gayer and happier.

"Well, you see," she replied, "we really need a sitting-room apiece under the new arrangement, don't we?".

"What about a screen down the middle of the hall?" cried Billy, as though suddenly inspired.

"Oh, good!" said Archie.

"But," Peg put in doubtfully, "that will necessitate whispering."

They all pondered for a moment. The matter was one that deserved great attention and consideration.

Archie broke the silence in his most practical manner, although coming forward with no ingenious suggestion.

"Yes," he said, "there's no doubt about it, the place is too small."

Peg laughed involuntarily. She did not catch Viola's expression of annoyance and resentment.

"Awkward, very," said Billy, swallowing a mouthful of cigarette smoke with much quiet enjoyment.

"But how could any of us tell when we took this place that we were going to set to partners?" asked Viola generally.

"That's it," said Billy. "Ah, how true it is that the ways of Providence are inscrutable— and very sportin'."

Hay's lips tightened and both his hands became fists. He dared not permit himself to look in the direction of his friend.

Instinctively knowing what was passing through Archie's mind Peg hurried into the pause. "I've got an idea," she cried.

"Have you, though!"

"You have so many brilliant ideas, dear," said Viola; "it's wonderful."

Peg's eyes were alight. "Billy can tell us, because he's an expert. Billy, do you think we could make a sitting-room of the coal-shed?"

Billy shifted his shoulders uneasily. An inveterate chaffer, he detested to be chaffed. "Oh Lord, yes," he said, "for you and Archie."

The knowledge that she had annoyed her husband gave Peg a momentary gleam of pleasure. He deserved so thoroughly well to be annoyed. Again her face was turned up towards Archie's.

"*You* wouldn't mind sitting in the dark with *me*, would you?"

Archie rose to the occasion nobly, but with an effort. "Where you are there also is my light."

" You darling," whispered Peg clearly, hiding a laughing face behind both Archie's hands.

Billy was not quite so much amused as he thought that he was going to be. Viola, on the contrary, was not amused at all.

" Well," said Billy, " I vote we call in an architect and have a room built on."

" That's all very well," said Viola, " but what are we to do in the meantime ? "

Archie obeyed Peg's silent appeal to keep up the ridiculous rally. " Exactly," he hurried to say. " That's the trouble, isn't it, Baby ? "

" It's no trouble to me," said Peg. " If I were doomed to spend the remainder of my life in a waiting-room on the Great Western Railway, I should still feel alone in the world with you."

In a manner of speaking Viola took the ball and returned it. " And that's how we feel, isn't it, Willy ? "

" Rather ! But "—Billy sank his voice—" for the Lord's sake don't call me Willy."

" Still," said Peg, " I think that perhaps it would be as well if we drew up a time-table."

" A time-table ! " Viola showed particular interest.

" Well, you see, we are really and truly honey-moon couples, aren't we ? "

" Of course we are."

The two men heard these remarks with horror.

" So far as the day goes it's all quite easy, Viola. We two can arrange to breakfast here after you two, as usual ; then you two can immediately go out, as usual ; and we two can have this room till luncheon, as usual."

" Quite, quite good," commented Viola.

" Toppin'," added Billy.

" Then," continued Peg, " you two can lunch alone, as usual ; while we two go round the course, as usual ; and leave you two in sole possession till tea-time, as usual. Do you see ? "

" A delightful distribution," replied Viola enthusiastically. " Quite as delightful as—as usual."

A curious sensation of mental weariness crept over Peg. From the moment that Archie had confessed himself at the breakfast-table as jealous her brain had been at work devising, planning, dissecting. She had had not only to bear her own burden, but Archie's as well. She constantly had had to exert all her powers of persuasion to keep Archie up to playing his part in what was to both a distasteful business. And when, after having been simulating for many hours a character that was entirely different from her own, she had been buoyed up with the belief that all further need for acting was at an end, it was a very hard thing to find that all her work had gone for nothing.

She knew that she had put very little spirit into the absurd but difficult scene she had just played. Nothing seemed to distress Viola, and for once Peg did not see through Billy's audacious bluffing.

" Quite as delightful as usual," repeated Viola.

" Yes, but the evening remains," said Billy.

" Exactly," added Viola, " there's the evening."

" Yes," said Hay heavily, " there's the evening."

Peg made a supreme effort. " Well, never say die. In the evening we must either take it in turns to use this room, or, if we are all here, must sit back to back."

Viola again went one better. " Of course," she said in her most matter-of-fact voice, " the natural solution of the difficulty is that either you two or we two say ' good night ' early."

" Quite so, quite so," said Billy.

Peg rose. She pined for air. She ached to get away to some quiet corner and sit alone.

" Or," she said, " if the nights are as fine as
t one is we could sit out."

" Of course ! " cried Viola. " But where ? "

" I'll go and see," said Peg.

Paying no attention to Hay's signals of distress, she left the room quickly.

Viola wondered why. " What about erecting
an arbour facing the moon ? " she asked, and
followed to find out.

CHAPTER XI

FOR the second time that evening the two men
had the hall to themselves. But the tables
had been turned. Archie was no longer the
generous victor who could afford to be kind to
a vanquished foe. Billy now occupied this
enviable position.

Hutton in a sulk was not a pleasant companion. He was either distressingly lugubrious
or excessively snappy. Hutton when pleased
with himself, and therefore with the world at
large, was almost too pleasant. He laughed constantly when a smile would have served the
same purpose. He was busy and exuberant and
noisy. In all moods he was a man whose temperament made itself felt. Being a gregarious

person who, having no hobbies and no power of concentration, disliked being alone, he was incapable of removing himself and working off depression or bad temper. He always was filled with an unconscious desire to stand in the limelight, to accept the centre position upon his particular stage. Mostly, it is true, he was pleased with himself, and so to most people he was dear old Billy Hutton, the breezy, the jovial, the rattling good fellow.

Hay knew him and all his moods, or rather, in both his moods, and was, or had been, affectionately disposed towards him always. But when the two wives had left the hall and he caught Billy's beaming smile, he began to wonder how it was that he had ever been his friend.

Hay never sulked. Life was too short. He could not afford the time that sulking demanded. When put out he became brusque and irritable. As a rule, he kicked whatever inanimate matter lay near to his foot, and immediately looked about for some small, but useful job that would keep his hands occupied. He would clean a gun, or splice a rod, or tidy up his desk.

7

At this moment he seized upon a jigger. The leather on its shaft had come loose. He would make it right, hoping that Billy would follow the women.

Not so Billy. He told himself that he was top dog this time and would make the most of it. So with a large cigar in one corner of his mouth and his hands deep in his pockets he took up a graceful, lazy attitude near Archie and watched him at work.

Meakin found Sir William Hutton and Major Hay in this position. He was extremely surprised.

" I have packed your things as instructed, Sir William," he said.

Archie looked up quickly. " Are you leaving here ? "

" Early to-morrow, sir," said Meakin, without giving Billy time to reply. " Sir William sleeps at the ' Cat and Fiddle ' in the village to-night, sir.'

" Is that so ? " asked Archie.

" Oh, no," replied Billy airily. " Oh, bless you, no. I told Meakin to pack my things for the same reason that you used to take your company out signallin'—just to give him something to do. Time hangs doocid heavy on Meakin's hands in this little place."

Meakin proved his mastery of the art of facial expression.

" How soon would you like me to unpack, Sir William ? " he said quietly.

" As soon as you like ; as soon as you like."

" Thank you, Sir William."

Billy's insouciance under what might have been awkward circumstances pleased Meakin very much. He waited until he was well inside the kitchen and then he laughed. The cook, who was a glutton for the glowing details of all the horrors of the week that is supplied to the lower classes in the form of Sunday newspapers, ticked him off as " an hysterical."

" I often do these little things," said Billy. " Must keep those sort of fellers up to concert pitch." He held out his cigar-case. " Try one of these, old boy."

" I don't think I'll smoke just now, thanks."

" Wise man. I wish I could do with fewer. Jolly bad things, cigars They not only carve a hole in one's pocket, but they knock a hole in one's wind." He flicked his ash into the fire-place expertly.

"You do smoke too much," said Archie shortly. He cut off a piece of twine with a serviceable penknife.

"No one knows that better than I do, but that's one of the first things that Vi's goin' to see to, she tells me. I shall be a changed man soon. My best pals won't know me. Ah, she is one in a' million, is Vi. Oh, but of course you know, don't you?"

Archie turned his back. "It's a fine night," he said.

Some of Billy's enjoyment was spoilt because there was no one in the room who knew how matters stood to see how well he was playing up. He would, at any rate, have lots to tell Peg that night.

"Yes, it's one of the best we've had," he replied. "By Jove, it was a brainy notion of mine that we should share this cottage, don't you think so?"

"As cottages go, yes, it's very conveniently planned."

Billy walked round his friend, so that he could watch the work. "I meant from the social point of view."

"Oh?"

" I'm ready to give any odds that if you hunted
for six months you wouldn't find four people
who rub along so well together."

Archie made no reply.

Billy insisted on having a reply. " What ?
Don't you agree ? " he added.

" Yes," said Archie. " It's quite remarkable."

For a moment or two Billy said nothing more.
He paused to enjoy the effect of his ragging.
It amused him to hear the usually imperturbable
Archie biting his words and only repressing an
angry outburst with difficulty.

" I can't get over it," he went on in his most
friendly and confidential manner. " Take me.
I've known any number of women, and at one
time was quite fond of Peg. You remember,
of course ? "

" Oh yes, I remember."

" But I've just discovered that the things one
knows most about are the things one knows least
about. What I mean is, oneself d'y'see, and life,
and so on. I don't mind tellin' you in confidence that I've just surprised myself tremendously. In fact, frankly—and after all, as you
said this mornin', and said jolly well too, frankness is the keynote of this foursome—I wouldn't

have believed myself capable of doin' what I've done. Would you ? "

This time Archie answered promptly, " No."

" Exactly," said Billy. " I'm glad you agree."

He crossed the hall slowly, helped himself to a liberal amount of whisky, shot in the lithia water, and drank.

" Have one ? " he asked.

" Thanks, no."

Billy only just managed to stop a loud laugh. This was the only time during the day that Archie allowed himself to drink whisky. He rarely missed this one.

" Gad," thought Billy, " he is in a shockin' wax, dear old fellow."

Then, with an even more irritating friendliness, he returned to his old position, and there was a slight note of patronage in his voice when he continued his endless stream of chatter.

" I think you'll like Peg, old man," he said.

Archie nearly lost his self-control. " I have always liked her. I think she's one of the best women I have ever met."

" Oh, thanks," replied Billy ; " thanks most awfully."

" Why do you thank me ? "

Billy shrugged his shoulders modestly. " Well, after all, y'see, I—I dare say I had something to do with shapin' her character, what ? "

Archie snorted. No twine had ever been wound so tight before.

" She's a sportsman too, is Peg. By Jove, she is. You'll find that, old man. I mean she understands the art of turning a blind eye in the true Nelsonian way. In fact, she's the very one for you."

Archie wished that he had cultivated sarcasm. " It's very kind of you to say so, I'm sure," he said.

" Not a bit," replied Billy graciously. " And dear little Vi, eh ? "

" Well ? "

" Well, it's a real pleasure to know that I shall make her happy for the first time in her life."

Billy had saved up this remark He regarded it as one of his best efforts. He expected to see Archie wince.

He was not disappointed. Archie not only winced as though he had been lashed across the face with a whip, he threw the club into a corner, wheeled round and marched over to the fire-place. But that was the only sign he let Billy see of the sting of his remark. That, and the sudden glint of his eyes.

Like a schoolboy Billy could not resist the temptation of carrying on his ragging until he drew his victim. He followed Archie slowly, sat on the back of a chair, crossed his feet, and eyed the long split tongues of his shoes thoughtfully. He now began to talk about himself with a mixture of admiration and disgust.

"It seems to me," he said slowly, as though the truth had just dawned upon him, "that I've got through life up to now like a boat without ballast. I mean, I've been devilish selfish and self-indulgent and that sort of thing. W. Hutton has been the star turn, so to speak, and everybody else the harmless necessary paddin'. I dunno how it is, but somehow or other I don't seem to have realised that life's—well, a pretty serious thing. Eh? I have just run through the days as a—a passenger train goes on. I mean I've stopped because I've had to at each station, so to speak, and passed on—what's the word?— automatically. Now, you know, old man, that's all right for a time. On you go in the same old way, stokin' up and so forth, superficially glancin'

at things on the line ; you get a bit careless
because you fancy you know all there is to be
known, and then comes a crash. By Jove, yes !
Then comes a crash ! If you get out of it with a
whole skin the obvious thing to do is—well, not
to do it again."

He laughed, but immediately returned to a
portentous, almost comic seriousness. He felt
that he was expressing himself very brilliantly.
He felt that he was saying things that ought
not to be wasted. He was indeed almost talking himself into believing that what he was
saying about himself was true.

Archie seethed. If Billy had looked at his eyes
he would have seen that only a few more such
minutes were required to bring about a much more
serious draw than he had started out to achieve.

But Billy continued to look at the hideously
decorative tongues of his shoes.

" In fact," he continued, " I may say that I'm
awake. I'm goin' to try very hard to be—well,
different. I shied at sayin' better, though goodness knows I oughtn't to—me, of all jokers. I'm
goin' to do my level to be worthy of Vi. That's
what I'm goin' to try and do. Don't you think
I'm right, old man ? "

He looked up with wide eyes, full of bland innocence.

"It seems to me," snapped Archie, "that you're quoting from the novels of emotional nursery governesses. I didn't think they were much in your line."

"Ah," replied Billy gravely, though inwardly he was laughing. "When a man has won the love of a very beautiful woman, he spouts nonsense for very joy."

"So it seems."

Archie's amazing self-control filled Billy with real admiration. Except for an occasional small sign, he did not seem to be having the smallest effect upon his old friend. It was quite remarkable, looking to the fact that no rag had been more excellently well carried out.

Billy, who soon grew tired of mental efforts, began to be rather annoyed. This continued calm on Archie's part was, he considered, a slight. He had taken a good deal of trouble to think out all the things that he had said, and he considered that they were good enough to win appreciation. He always had considered Archie a little dense, and he made up his mind to adopt a broader method. He intended to draw Archie, however far he was obliged to go. In the back of his head was the remembrance of a most unhappy morning, a most humiliating afternoon, and an offensively bad dinner at the " Cat and Fiddle " in the evening. The coal-shed had a nasty place in his memory also. All these things he debited to Archie's account.

" You may have noticed," he said, " that I've taken to callin' you old man again."

" It hasn't escaped me," Archie replied. " Don't do it if it costs you an effort."

" An effort ? Good Lord, no ! The fact is, dear old man, I am at peace with the world, and I don't want to see you out in the cold."

" It's very kind of you, I'm sure."

" Not a bit. After all, we're old and dear pals, and but for you I never should have met Vi."

Still no sign of the anger that Billy wished to see. However, he had not done yet. He was determined to get his own back for the fright that he had received from Archie in the morning. He left his chair, stood with his back to the fire-place, and dug Archie in the ribs with his elbow.

" You're a deep dog," he laughed.

Archie removed himself out of range of the

elbow. "I dislike being nudged," he said, "if you don't mind my saying so."

"Oh, a very, very deep dog," continued Billy. "All the while I've been making the running with Vi, you've been quietly spreading your bird-lime for Peg."

Hay was too furiously angry to speak.

"I don't blame you," said Billy, without any knowledge of what he was momentarily bringing nearer. "Peg's just your sort. As for Vi, she's a darling. It's quite extraordinary how she's cottoned on to me. Mind you, I didn't start it. She led me on, you know, what?"

Archie could stand no more. His self-control left him in a flash. He whipped round upon Billy. His face was distorted with rage.

"How dare you talk of my wife like that?" he shouted.

"*Your* wife!" laughed Billy, his object achieved at last.

"Yes, my wife."

"But if she's your wife, where does my wife come in? Good Lord, do you want to start a harem?"

"I want no more of you," cried Archie. "Damn you, you're driving me to blasphemy.

I loathe the sight of you. I loathe the sound of your voice. You'd better get out quick or I shall hurt you. Are you going?"

" No."

" Then, by God, I'll make you."

He sprang at Billy and seized him by the collar. Billy tried to struggle free. He was almost lifted off his feet. He made a frantic effort to throw Archie off. A chair was upset with a crash.

Peg ran in quickly. " Archie, Archie," she cried. " What are you doing?"

At the sound of Peg's voice Archie recovered himself. He let Billy go and stood up straight, shaking from head to foot.

Viola hastened in. " What's the matter? What's happened?" she asked.

There was silence for a moment. Then Peg spoke calmly. " There seems to have been a rather unseemly quarrel," she said. " Evidently this place is not large enough to hold us all."

She turned to the two men. She saw Billy shoot a wink at Viola. She saw that Archie had again given himself away. It was therefore the right moment to play her last card.

" Archie," she said, " I think it's time we said

good-night." She lit two candles, kept one, and handed the other to Archie. He took it mechanically.

" Come, darling," she said.

She took his arm. Together they made their way towards the door.

" Where are you going ? " cried Billy.

" Where, William ? To my room, of course."

Appalled and horror-stricken, Viola watched them go, heard them mount the stairs, heard them enter the room above, and heard the key turned in the lock.

" Well ! " cried Billy.

But Viola was unable to speak. She looked as if she had been turned to stone.

CHAPTER XII

FOR the third time during this amazing day in the lives of the Hays and Huttons the tables had been turned. In the morning the victory lay with Lady Hutton and Archibald Hay. In the evening the entire position had been won by Viola Hay and William Hutton. How did this struggle to regain happiness stand now ?

Peg's bedroom was a small but pretty room.

Two oak-posted beds stood side by side. An oak dressing-table, quaintly and usefully designed, upon which all the paraphernalia of a wealthy woman's needs was laid out neatly, stood between two long, narrow windows which opened outwards and framed a wide rolling view, and caught the clean, sweet air whose breath was delicately flavoured with salt. One of its doors led out upon the passage, the other into a small dressing-room. There were two white canework chairs, large and comfortable, and everywhere the same note of colour met the eye gratefully. It was the room of a woman of great taste with the means to carry it out.

The unsteady wicks of two candles threw a dancing light upon all these things. One of the candles was held by Archie, the other by Peg.

Both of them stood near the door which Archie had just shut and locked. Both of them stood quite still as though posing for the photographer, and if some photographer had been able to snap them as they stood, the picture would have been one that would have given the student of facial expression some trouble to read.

The tall, fair, muscular man, clean of limb,

square of shoulder, had one hand on the handle
of the door. In the other was the candle, held
on a level with his eyes. The light it threw on
his face made plain an expression of anger,
disgust.

The beautiful, slight woman, her whole body
stiff with fright, stood near. The light of the
candle that was clutched by her with both hands
showed that her eyes were distended, her lips
slightly parted.

They might have been posing as Bluebeard and
Sister Anne's sister, illustrating that horrible
moment when the tyrant came upon the girl
whose curiosity had taken her into the forbidden
room.

A minute passed before Peg broke the pose.
Agitation made her breathing irregular. The
candle trembled in her hands.

" Oh, Archie ! " she whispered.

Hay's emotion made him brusque. " What
is it ? " he asked.

" Oh, Archie, Archie," repeated Peg.

" What's the matter now ? "

" I ought not to have brought you here."

" You said it was the right thing to do."

" I know. That was before we came. But

now I see that it's the wrong thing, utterly the
wrong thing."

" Why ? "

" Oh, don't you see ? Can't you see ? "
There were tears in Peg's eyes.

" No."

" I'm locked in my room with you ! "

Archie had received too many shocks during
the day to remember very much about the
amenities. His voice rang out sharply.

" Well, that's what you wanted."

Peg wrung one hand. " Yes, but now I'm
terrified."

She made a swift turn, crossed the room, put
the candle upon the dressing-table, put both
hands over her face, and whimpered like a child
who had climbed up a tree and was afraid to go
down.

Hay remained by the door. There was nothing
foolish or undignified in his attitude in what was
certainly a foolish and undignified position. He
looked grave and grim.

" I tell you," sobbed Peg, all her courage
deserting her, " that I'm terrified."

No word came from Hay. He had obeyed orders.
His silence and apparent lack of sympathy

added to Peg's terror. " I'm going out," she cried, and made a dash towards the door.

Hay retained the handle firmly. " No," he said.

" I must ! I will ! " cried Peg wildly.

" No, if you go down now all our work will go for nothing."

Peg clutched his arm and tried to pull his hand away from the handle.

" Please, please, Archie," she begged. " I have never been locked in a room with anyone before. I can't stand it."

Hay never budged. He was rock-like.

" No. We're here, and whatever comes of it, we stay here."

Peg tugged his arm. She was crying bitterly. She looked charmingly young and helpless.

" How dare you talk to me like that ! I never would have helped you if I'd thought that you were a bully, never ! "

" Keep your nerve," said Hay quietly.

" What's the use of keeping my nerve when I'm losing my reputation ! . . . Oh, let me go ; let me go."

If a third person, a stranger to both these people, knowing nothing of what had happened, could have watched this scene from the dressing-room he would have found in it much that was irresistibly comic, just as the third person, coming suddenly upon people in a state of agitation with no reason to feel sympathetic, always must first see the comic side which agitation invariably possesses.

Hay put the candle on a chair and his hand on Peg's shoulder.

"You've been an angel of pluck to-day," he said. "You kept me reasonable when I had lost my self-control. Mostly to help me you are doing something that I shall never forget, whether it's successful or not. It's the only thing we can do. Let's see it through together."

Peg's sobs came more quietly. "Saying sweet things to me in an almost dark room doesn't alter the position. Think what everyone will say?"

"It's not a pleasant position," said Hay, "but it was a Napoleonic idea. Stop crying, please."

Peg made no further attempt to capture the handle. She moved away, hunted here and there for a handkerchief, found one, and began to dab her scalding cheeks.

"It's one thing to have Napoleonic ideas and quite another to carry them out."

She sat down limply. Gradually her sobs

ceased. But she was very nearly tired out. She never had undergone so many varying emotions in the course of one short day. Hay's quiet authority and determination, however, soothed and strengthened her. After all, Archie was right. Billy, notwithstanding his severe lesson, had fallen under Viola's spell again, and Viola herself was entirely shameless. Peg well knew that she had devised an almost devilishly ingenious and convincing scheme for bringing the erring pair to their senses, if they were to be brought to their senses at all. Yes, Archie was right. It must be seen through. There was no going back.

" Won't you light some more candles ? " she asked, feeling rather ashamed of her tears.

Archie nodded. With heavy tread he marched across the room and put a match to a candle which stood on a table at the foot of Billy's bed. Its wick was short and it took light reluctantly. Archie was very patient. He displayed no irritation.

" Thank you," said Peg. " Not any more."

" Why not ? "

" These candles burn quickly, and we may need the others."

" Exactly," he said.

" I wouldn't be in the dark for anything on earth," she added.

" Nor I," said Archie.

Hay wondered vaguely what he was to do with himself. He looked about hoping to find something that he could mend, something upon which he could work with his hands. There seemed to be nothing. He wandered aimlessly about the room. He examined the books. They were mostly rather charmingly got up reprints of the standard poets. He couldn't stand poetry. He thought it somewhat poisonous stuff. He took up a slim volume called " The Cloud of Witness," and read a page or two of it solemnly. It seemed to him to be very useful, just the thing to be in the bedroom of a good woman. But he put it back in its place carefully.

Then he made a slow tour of the room and stood for several minutes before the half-dozen pictures that hung from a rail upon the matting-covered walls. One showed a young nude figure pressing impotently against a great resisting door. He didn't understand it. He noticed that the muscle of the left leg was wrongly placed. He moved away.

Another represented nearly the whole of the figure of a very beautiful girl with her hair flying behind her. She was evidently taking her dog for a walk in her father's park, although why she should be permitted by her mother to do so in what was an extremely careless arrangement of clothing—the whole of one shoulder was bare, an extremely pretty shoulder—he couldn't think. Evidently very foolish people, her parents. And the dog! Never in his time had he seen any dog with such legs. Bad work.

He passed to a third. It showed a man and a girl in classical garments standing in a theatrical attitude of uncomfortable love-making in what appeared to be an archway. At a rough calculation he made out the man to be eight feet five, and the girl seven foot, both without stockings. If that's Art, he thought, give him a sporting calendar.

He took a look at another. At a first glance, without wishing to be over-critical—bad or good, he was not able to do anything of the kind, thank God—he saw that the Roman soldier, who seemed to be rather keen on applause, was represented with the scabbard of his short sword on his right hip. " Good Lord ! " he thought.

He decided to cut the last one.

Again at a loose end, he turned away from the wall and examined a rack of boots and shoes, all spotless and gleaming, and carefully jacked. He knew that they were Billy's. He was annoyed. He considered it in extremely bad taste to have a rack of boots in a woman's room. He was annoyed also because he always had considered Billy's boots to be wrong. They were good boots, well made and well kept. But they were, to his mind, a trifle over-smart. They caught the eye. Some had drab uppers with white buttons, others brown leather uppers, and there were dress boots with dull black cloth uppers. He never had been able to see the necessity for uppers of any kind other than leather. Nor had he ever been able to see the point of elaborate puncturing and patterns on brown shoes. He relegated those things to the people he called precious—the people who went in for waisted coats, wore their hats at an angle, and were never seen out of pretty-pretty ties which women called tweeky.

As he stood looking at this offending rack he remembered that he had labelled Billy a precious dresser for many years. He remembered staying

with him at old Sir William's place for the shooting almost immediately after he came home on
his first leave from India. He had not seen
Billy for some years. He did not say anything
about the clothes he came down in the first
morning, but they had made him blink. They
seemed to him to be altogether overdone. One
or two civilians actually had said at breakfast,
" Hello, Billy, who's your tailor ? " If they had
been in the Service and Billy had been in the
Service, they would not have made that remark
and Billy would not have worn such clothes.

Hay was one of those men who was a little self-
conscious among a collection of human beings.
Good form was his fetish. In order not to be
conspicuous he wore clothes of the same cut
and much the same material as the clothes he
had worn when he first ordered clothes for himself, and accordingly was far more conspicuous
than the man who permitted his tailor to dress
him. He was out of date. In many ways he
allowed good form to make him uncomfortable.
He never, for instance, would walk up Bond
Street in anything but a silk hat, whether in
the morning or the afternoon. Nor would he
dream of dining at his Senior Service Club out

of evening clothes, in or out of season. He kept up his membership of a jovial little club in Piccadilly, at which he turned up his nose, for the sole purpose of being able to get dinner in dittoes. Even with dittoes he never yet had worn brown shoes in London, nor a soft shirt, any more than he would be seen in the country in a stiff white shirt and black shoes. Good form demanded of him certain things and they had to be done, whatever the discomfort and trouble. Civilians might be as lax as they cared to be, whoever they were. No laxity for him. He was a very sterling character.

No wonder that he found it excessively uncomfortable to be forced to spend hours locked into the bedroom of a woman who was not his wife. No wonder that he endeavoured, being there for what he took to be a good reason, to ignore as far as possible the fact that it was the bedroom of a woman who was not only not his wife, but the wife of the man who had been his best friend.

His manner, as he prowled carefully about the room, was admirable. He might have been in the stationery department of the Army and Navy Stores. He was good form personified. And yet he was undergoing great mental agony in regard to his wife's sudden misdemeanour. Indeed, he never before had suffered so keenly, and never before had reproached himself so bitterly. As a matter of fact suffering, until that day, had not been known by him, nor had he ever had cause to reproach himself.

Peg watched him. At first she watched him without knowing that she was watching him. She was so tired, so dispirited, so disappointed. Obsessed with the knowledge that she had failed to bring about a new and happy understanding between Viola and Archie, she was only aware vaguely that someone was moving about the room slowly. Directly she had sat down, almost for the first time that day, a sensation of physical exhaustion came upon her. She forgot for the time the awkwardness, the compromising nature of the position into which she had deliberately placed herself and Hay. All that she could think about was that she was oh so tired, so weary, so worn out. She felt that she never again would be able to move out of her chair. She felt without hope, without spirit, without energy. And it was very reasonable that she should feel in this way. A beautiful woman had fallen in love with, and completely fascinated her husband. So far as she knew, that was the position of affairs. It was perfectly true that she had not interfered hitherto with Billy's numerous small flirtations. That was not saying that she cared no longer for Billy. On the contrary, under her sane and wise system of remaining happy though married, it showed that her love for him had much unselfishness and consideration. It made her extremely unhappy, therefore, to believe that Billy's love for her had become so attenuated as to allow him to feel fascinated by another woman.

She knew so well all dear old Billy's little weaknesses. She loved him as much for these as for his sound points, as all good women do. She knew how enormously Viola's obvious passion —it seemed the only word—would appeal to his vanity. How could she tell what might not happen while he was under her spell? She knew that he would win her forgiveness. She knew that she would take him back under whatever circumstances he came to her. He was as much her child as her husband, because, as she was the stronger character of the two, he would be at a loose end without her in his life.

All these things went through her mind as she sat listlessly looking into the unsteady flame of the candle, not yet having recovered from her breakdown at finding herself locked into her room with Archie. But presently, as her nerves steadied themselves, she became aware that the person who moved about her room was Archie, and she began to watch him with interest.

She noticed the studied impersonal attitude that he adopted. She saw him endeavouring to make himself interested in her pictures which she knew had no sort of appeal. She saw him stand silently in front of Billy's boots, and interpreted quite correctly the things that he thought about them. She saw him seize eagerly upon the poker, the head of which was loose, and with great earnestness screw it tight. She saw him then gaze wistfully about with an almost pathetic desire to find something with which to occupy himself.

To her astonishment, Peg found herself smiling. The sense of humour which had carried her through several other unhappy moments was creeping through her misery. Very much against her will, she began to see the funny side of her position, the absurdity of having been uncomfortable, even in her bedroom, alone with such a man as Archie was, a man so straight, so scrupulous, so prim, so conventional. And no sooner had she realised this than she began to piece together the thoughts that she knew must be passing through Archie's brain. She wanted to laugh and she wanted to cry. But above all, she wanted to know what effect her sudden manœuvre had upon Viola and Billy.

CHAPTER XIII

PEG got up suddenly, went over to one of the windows, threw it open and looked out.

There was a full moon. Golden and opulent it hung in a sparkling, cloudless sky. Its soft light threw a glamour upon all the silent earth. The downs near the cottage, unbroken by shadows, looked as though they had been powdered with fine snow. No trees broke the skyline. The waving line of hills seemed to touch the sky as the shore touches the sea. The sky, clear and blue, might have been the sea, and the stars that peppered its surface a great fleet of boats at anchor, all with their lights. No sound came through the singing silence except the low whispering of a gentle breeze.

For some little time Peg remained at the window, watching and listening, enchanted. She felt that she must hold her breath, that it was right even to think in a whisper. She smiled ever so faintly when the breeze puffed against her face. The moon and the stars seemed, like herself, to be the only things awake in a sleeping world. As she stood there her optimism returned. There was nothing wrong with the world. It was too fine a setting to be made ugly by mere human creatures, by their quarrels and passions, vanities and spites. All *must* come right, she assured herself.

She left the world and went back to life. There was Archie leaning grimly and patiently upon an oak chest, and below in the hall were Viola and Billy. Surely it would be their fault if life did not continue to be good.

Peg's spirits took an upward turn. She felt refreshed and inspired. She began to regain some of her characteristic confidence in herself. She wanted to talk and have companionship.

So she drew forward the other arm-chair. " You look so uncomfortable, Archie," she said. " Do sit down."

" Thank you," said Archie. He sat stiffly.

Peg sat also, and heaved a little sigh. " These chairs might be worse, mightn't they ? "

" Yes. But it doesn't matter."

" Don't you mind ? "

" No."

" I do," said Peg, making a face. " We may have to sit in them all night." She waited for Hay to say something. She ached for him to become conventional. He remained silent.

" I don't think," she added, " that even our worst enemies can say that we are not doing our best. . . . Do you, Archie ? "

" No," he said.

She waited for more. She waited in the hope that he would find something cheery and helpful to say. But no ; he had finished.

She tried again.

" I do think that we deserve to succeed. Don't you, Archie ? "

" Yes," he said.

" If people were to judge by appearances we shouldn't have a *friend* in the world . . . should we, Archie ? "

" No," he said.

" It only shows how cruel it is to judge by appearances, doesn't it, Archie ? "

" Yes," he said.

Peg began to move her foot. Archie's laconic answers did not help to make conversation easy. It would have been better if sometimes he had disagreed with her. She kept patient.

" If only we could hear some sound below," she began again. " They seem so quiet. If only Billy would do something, that would give us some idea of how he is feeling. If only he would break something. Then we should know for certain that he was upset. He always breaks something when he is upset." She paused. " I beg your pardon ? "

Archie was gazing at his boot.

" I thought you said something," said Peg.

" No," he said.

" I beg your pardon."

Peg's patience was running out. She shot an irritable glance at Archie. She wished mightily that he was not quite such an admirable person. She almost wished that she could make him annoyed with her. And yet, after all, that was not a kind thing to wish. Poor old Archie ! No wonder he found it difficult to make conversation. Yesterday at this time he was lying full stretch on a bear's skin studying Braid's book on golf, with a good light behind his shoulder, and a pipe between his teeth, with a delightful view of Viola whenever he found time to take it. To-night where was his book, his pipe, and where was Viola?

She wondered what, under similar conditions, Billy would have done. He certainly would not have been sitting like a man on a court-martial, straight-backed. He would have been talking. Oh yes, he would have had plenty to say, plenty that was melodramatic, picturesque, and slightly slangy.

" Don't you think that Billy ought to be upset by this time, Archie ? " she asked.

" Yes."

She was unable to keep pathos out of her voice. " I do wish you would say two words for a change."

" Very well," said Archie.

" Thank you ! " she said.

And then there was silence.

CHAPTER XIV

WHEN Billy, having heard the key turn in the lock of his wife's room, whipped round upon Viola to be encouraged by her in his belief that this last move on the part of Peg and Hay belonged to their scheme as it had been explained to him by Viola, his question died on his lips.

It was not the beautiful, stately, confident, somewhat supercilious Viola whom he found, not the calm, assured, charmingly mannered woman of the world whom he had known intimately for years, but a woman with her face distorted with jealousy, rage, and an almost tigerish desire for revenge.

He found her with her hands pressed over her mouth as if to force back a shriek. He saw that her face flamed, her eyes blazed, and the veins swelled upon her temples. The well-bred woman, whose training and environment had taught her to think of outward appearances even when under the influence of the strongest emotion, had become the primeval woman, lusting to give full vent to her feelings, obsessed with the desire to wound, to hurt.

Billy was shocked. To his way of thinking, women always should be pleasant to the eye, smiling, restful, graceful. Never had he seen any woman so much out of control as this one except once. He had been motoring through Italy, and one morning was waiting in the yard

of a village hotel for the car, and had seen a
peasant woman catch sight suddenly of another
who had, it was said, tempted her sweetheart
away. She had entered the yard with a basket
of eggs and vegetables on her arms, a bright-
eyed, smiling, sunburnt, pretty creature; but
in an instant she became a virago. Dropping her
basket, she had given an animalish cry, sprung
upon her enemy, flung her down, and was stamp-
ing upon her before she could be seized and
carried away.

Billy was thankful that Peg was safely locked
into her room. He was also completely amazed
at Viola's unexpected change. He went over
to her, in a kindly manner, and put his hand on
her shoulder. It was a characteristic gesture of
his.

"My dear child," he said, "what is it?
What's the matter? This is a part of their
game. We've done so well that they had to do
this. It means nothing—does it?"

Viola flung his hand away, and turned on him
fiercely.

"You fool!" she cried, "you fool!"

Billy staggered back. "I say!" he said
feebly, "I say!"

" Can't you see what it means ? Are you so blind that you can't see what it means ? "

" Yes, I am."

Billy replied with a touch of temper. To be called a fool was a new thing. To be hissed at angrily and have scornful questions flung at his head were methods to which he was quite unaccustomed.

" Tah ! " said Viola, with something that was neither a laugh nor a sob. She flung up her hands and commenced to pace the room. Every now and then she pulled up irresolutely by the door as though about to go. Then she turned into the room again and went wildly up and down.

The swish of her dress as she went, the inarticulate sounds that she made, the way in which she clasped and beat her hands filled Billy with a queer feeling of uneasiness. It was not in him to concentrate and argue, to feel his way point by point to a reasonable conclusion. He was constitutionally unable to switch his mind quickly from one line of thought to another. The machinery of his body was in good enough order, but his brains were rusty. He never had used them because he never had been obliged or called upon to use them.

And so he stood where Viola had left him and watched her, appalled at what he called her temper, amazed at what seemed to him to be an exhibition of bad form such as he would have sworn was impossible in a woman of Viola's birth and bringing up.

" Why ? " he kept on asking inwardly. " Why ? She said that . . . It was her idea to . . . she deliberately asked . . . absolutely proved that they were . . . It beats me, upon my soul, it does. Look at her. Just look at her ! The temper of a . . . a tigress, goin' on as if she were in a cage. What's the idea ? What's it all for—all about ? By gad, she nearly had me over, dashin' me off like that ! I didn't want to touch her. Good Lord, that's all done with ! I just wanted to let her see that there was a man present whose advice and that sort of thing was to be had and welcome for the asking ! . . . Up and down, up and down—she'll swish something over in a moment. . . . She's off. No she's not. What a poisonous temper. All buck half an hour ago. Top dog, by a long way. Now she looks absolutely biffed up. Why ? That's what I want to know. Why ? . . . If she's altered her mind about the whole

blessed thing why the devil can't she say so and
get me to put it right? Seems so odd—goin'
on like this. Actin'! that's what she's doin'!
Yes, that's what it is. She's actin'. She don't
really think there's anything wrong—good Lord,
she can't, she had the position clear enough just
now, but she's givin' herself the satisfaction of
thinkin' that it's wrong and is in a sort of way
enjoyin' it. Oh, I dunno. It beats me! . . .
Now she's off. What's she goin' to do? Knock
on the door? Own that she's beaten? Cry
on Archie's neck? . . . No. There she goes
again, up and down, up and down. Dashed if
it doesn't make me all dizzy. And why, eh?
What's the good of bein' a Lady Macbeth if
there isn't a damned spot, or whatever it was?"

With his slightly thinning hair perfectly
smooth except where it went naturally into
thick smooth kinks, with his moustache properly
twisted away from his lip, his well-shaped eyebrows undisturbed, his well-cut features unruffled,
there stood Billy, wide-eyed, apparently not
more than usually interested in what was going
on. His hands were thrust deep into the pockets
of the admirably cut golf coat that he had worn
all day. His legs, in wide breeches which had

been very carefully designed and carried out, and were entirely successful, were planted firmly. No one would have imagined that dozens of elementary questions framed in ordinary every-day language were rushing through his head, that he was rapidly becoming more and more irritable, more and more nervous.

He spoke aloud finally.

"Look here, you know, Viola, you'll get tired soon."

"Tired! tired!" she echoed, walking faster.

"Why not—well, sit down?"

She snapped at him. "You can sit if you can," she said.

"If I can?" thought Billy. "What a weird thing to say. What the deuce——"

He began to feel the necessity of fidgeting with something. He found a solitary wax match in his pocket and commenced to worry it unconsciously. He noticed, with quite disproportionate indigna-tion, that a spoon had been left on the dresser.

"What does she mean by if I can?"

A happy idea struck him. He would mix a whisky-and-soda. He told himself that, for no reason that he knew, he might be all the better shortly for a little stimulant. He walked over to the dresser and helped himself, making more noise than he need have done in putting down the bottle. The atmosphere was so highly charged with an emotion that he was unable to understand that a commonplace, everyday noise soothed him.

He felt more inclined to demand from Viola an explanation of her disagreeable treatment of him. He turned towards her and found to his immeasurable relief that she was no longer pacing the room. It was true that her attitude was tragic, but at least she was standing still.

" I think they're carryin' their idiotic joke a bit too far, don't you ? " he asked.

Apparently Viola did not hear him. He repeated his remark with more voice.

Viola looked up at him with a steady, disconcerting gaze. She did not seem so much to be looking at him as in him. She did not catch his eyes. She seemed to examine his forehead, his chin, his eyebrows, then his soft collar and tie, and finally she dwelt for a moment on his shoes. She scoffed, turned away, sat down in a chair at the card table, and upon this she put her two beautiful pointed elbows and leaned forward with her face between her long, slim hands.

Billy considered her manner most peculiar, most unpleasant, most uncalled-for. What had he done, he should like very much to know, to be treated as though he were an impudent upholsterer's man come to hang curtains? He could only see that he had played the fool extremely well in order to help her to awaken her husband at her urgent request.

" Upon my soul, Viola," he spluttered, " you really might be a little less cryptic."

" Don't," she said.

" Don't what ? " asked Billy.

Viola shifted in her chair, so that he might not see her face. " I strongly advise you to leave me alone," she said.

" Well ! "

For the moment that was all that Billy could find to say. This was gratitude, was it ? This was all the thanks he got for frightening Peg into taking Archie up to her room, for being fallen upon by a man three inches taller than himself, and for having been made to spend, before these things happened, a day that he was not likely to forget for a considerable time ? The unkindness of Viola's treatment rankled in his mind, but not so painfully as the weird manner in which she was behaving after what he could only regard as her second decisive victory, largely brought about by himself. His uneasiness increased snowball fashion. The more he rolled things over in his mind the larger became his nervousness. In his turn, he began to pace up and down. He stopped every now and then to listen for any sounds from the room above. He threw irritable glances at the silent volcanic figure, with the bare shining arms and graceful shoulders.

" I'm damned if I can stand much more of this," he burst out at last.

He might have been talking to a mute. He made a swift movement, put his hands on the card table, and bent down towards Viola.

" What's the meanin' of all this, please ? I've a right to know, and I demand to know. . . . You may think it awfully clever and superior, and the Lord knows what, to play tragics all by yourself. It don't amuse me one atom. You've made a cat's-paw of me for days. You've pretty well rotted eight of 'em by monopolisin' me and by keepin' me away from golf and things. You've plunged me into a confoundedly unpleasant mix-up, and I resent it. Do you see ? I'm

sorry to talk like this, but you bring it on yourself. I shouldn't talk like this if you played the
game. *I've* played the game. And I shouldn't
be here now if you hadn't dragged not only me
but Peg too into your blessed row with Archie."

Viola sprang to her feet. " Cease pestering
me ! ", she cried.

" Pestering ! "

" If I had anything to say to you, I should
say it. I've nothing to say to you. I've
nothing to say to anybody. I want to think what
I'm going to do."

She went over to the fireplace quickly.

Billy's blood was up. He followed her. His
face was red. " But I've got something to say,
and it's this——"

" I don't want to hear."

" You shall hear. I deeply regret that I was
generous enough to help you."

" Generous ! "

" Yes, generous."

" Generous ! " she echoed scornfully. " You
hadn't the remotest notion until this evening
what I was making you do. Do you think I
should have chosen *you* if I hadn't known that
your egregious vanity would have made it im-

possible for you to see what I was using you for ?
You stand about like a waiter with his mouth
watering for a tip. You seem to think that your
wonderful acting demands favourable criticism.
You want me to fling bouquets at your feet.
You can't see for yourself, without goading me
and pestering me with your questions, that I've
been wasting my time, making a fool of myself
over a man who doesn't care about me."

" Do you mean me ? " cried Billy.

" You, you, you ! Are you the only man in
the world ? You twist everything round to yourself. Who should I mean but Archie ? "

Her voice broke. She put her handkerchief up
to her trembling lips.

" I don't understand a dash thing about any
of this," said Billy.

" You wouldn't be standing about as if you
were at a cricket match if you did," she replied.
" I've made a fool of myself. That's what makes
my blood boil as much as anything. I've been
the love-sick woman, planning and scheming to
get the man who was supposed to be in love with
me to love me more, and all the time he didn't
love me and hasn't loved me, but has been in
love with another woman."

" Do you mean Archie ? " stammered Billy.

" Yes ! Yes ! Yes ! Who should I mean if I don't mean Archie ? Oh, how blind I've been ! All this time I've been putting down his treatment of me to calm content. I was certain that he loved me, and all I wanted him to do was to say so. He must have left off loving me months ago—oh, my God, months ago ! "

Billy's mouth had gone dry. He could hardly speak. " Who—who do you think he loves now, then ? "

" Who ? " she replied shrilly, with a sort of laugh. " And yet I've been as blind as you've been. I suspected nothing any more than you did. Such friends—the four of us—going everywhere together, never happy when apart. No wonder ! Ah, how plain it all seems now. Dozens of times, when I would rather have been alone with Archie, he has said ' Let's get Peg and Billy.' ' Where are Peg and Billy ? ' And Peg, always so merry and cheery, always ready to walk round the links or stand on the bank, or join the luncheon party on the moors whatever the weather—Peg, whom I have known all my life. Oh, I never would have believed it of her."

Billy staggered.

" Peg ! " he cried. " Peg ! Archie in love with Peg ? "

" Yes, Peg—the straight, scrupulous Peg. He and she have had an understanding for months ! "

" It's a lie ! "

" Archie said so this morning ; we heard him, both of us, in this room."

" But—but you told me that——"

" I was hopelessly wrong. I gave Peg credit for too much cleverness. They had no scheme to make us ashamed. Why should they make us ashamed ? They didn't care about us. All they care about is themselves. They welcome what they take to be our foolishness. It has given them the chance they've waited for —the honourable people ! Archie said so, this morning."

Billy loosened his collar. His face was quite white.

" Peg in love with Archie," he managed to say. " Peg ! . . . You're talking bosh."

" You believed it this morning when you followed them everywhere."

" Yes, but I—I thought it over. It's impossible ! "

" Is it ? . . . Where are they now ? You

waste my time. Talking is done with for me.
You may do what you like. Grin and bear it,
mope and wring your hands, whatever you
think best. But I—oh, I'll make them pay for
this. There shall be no publicity, no scandal?
London shall echo with this story. They think
they're going to sail together, in speechless joy,
into a sort of private harbour of bliss, do they?
Well, they shall find that they've not got an Aunt
Martha to deal with in me. I go to London to-
morrow. I file a petition for divorce to-morrow."

She flung back her head, gathered up her dress,
and left the hall.

Billy caught up a Doulton-ware jug and flung
it into the grate. The crash echoed through the
room.

CHAPTER XV

" WHAT'S that?" asked Archie.

Peg jumped up with a cry of joy. " It's
Billy! He's broken something! Oh, Archie,
we're going to win, we're going to win after all."

She burst into tears. She cried like a mother
who having watched her boy only just escape a
bad accident among the traffic in the middle of
the road, sees him arrive safely on the pavement.

She cried noisily, giving little high-pitched sounds, as though her tears were not sufficiently relieving. And all the while she hunted here and there for her handkerchief.

Archie had risen. Peg's joyful outburst brought him to his feet eagerly. He found the missing handkerchief with mechanical politeness, and became aware that his companion in the horrible adventure had broken down. It was the first time that he had seen her in tears.

" Poor little soul," he thought. " She's tired out."

He crept to the door, bent down and listened. He distinctly heard steps on the stairs, the swish of a dress as someone passed the door. Then he heard a handle turned, and a door opened and shut. It was Viola.

All this while, then, she had been in the hall with Billy. He had been right when he thought that he had heard the rumble of voices. But evidently they had not been in the smallest degree perturbed by his exit with Peg. One or other of them long ago would have tried to force a way into the room. No. Peg was jumping to conclusions again. That crash was caused by a careless servant.

There was another crash.

Peg made a rush for the door. " I'm going out," she cried. " Billy may hurt himself."

Archie seized her wrist. " No," he said.

" Let me go. This is my room."

" Go and sit down."

The voice was very stern. Peg sobbed aloud, and went back into the room.

" I swore to carry out your plan," said Archie. " I have done my best to turn this tragedy into a comedy by trying to apply a sense of humour. We must stay where we are. We can't make things worse by staying," he said. " Because someone is breaking something you imagine that it must be Billy, because, as we both know, it is a habit of his to do so when put out. Forgive my saying so, but we thought that we were winning this afternoon, and we were—not right. If it should be Billy . . ."

He paused, as though to choose his words carefully. It was the natural result of barrack training.

" Well ? " she asked.

" Then," he continued, " there may be some small amount of hope."

Peg smiled involuntarily. Woman-like, she had made up her mind that there was no further reason to be frightened, that the bedroom scheme had succeeded. Archie's orderly-room caution amused her.

"Dear old Billy," she murmured, and set about drying away her tears.

Yes, they might as well remain in the bedroom now. But Peg suddenly became aware of the fact that her shoes were drawing her feet and that she was rather tightly laced.

"I suppose," she said tentatively, "there is no possibility of my being able to lie down."

"None whatever," replied Hay briskly.

"Perhaps you're right."

"There is no perhaps."

"Very well," said Peg. "Then we will remain uncomfortable. But I'm afraid I'm going to lose my temper. In fact, I'm sure I am. You're beginning to treat me as though I were a corporal."

"I'm sorry," said Hay. "Very sorry."

"Whenever I get into a temper—and it isn't often—somebody has to pay for it. This time it will be Billy and Viola. I'll stay here now until she and he have humbly apologised. That's settled."

"It's our only chance," said Hay, "especially if you are right about Billy."

"Oh, I'm right. Think of the things he's smashed. . . . Ha, ha!"

Hay turned and regarded her with astonishment. "Did I hear you laugh?"

"I believe so," said Peg. "I think I laughed. In fact, I think I am laughing now."

"But, forgive my saying so, is this the time for laughter?"

"Yes; don't you see the glimmer of light at the end of the tunnel?"

"Do you?"

"A distinct glimmer. It grows bigger and bigger."

Hay thought hard for a moment and then shook his head.

"I don't see it," he said.

Peg had not lost her temper after all. She was the old and cheery Peg again, Peg the optimist, Peg the ready-witted, Peg the confident. "The point is this," she said, smiling joyfully. "Billy is now quite sure that you and I are no better than we ought to be."

"Good Lord!"

"That's splendid, isn't it?"

"Is it?"

"Why, of course it is, dear man! That's why

we're here, you see. That being so, all we've got
to do is to convince Viola of this also."

" Is that necessary ? "

" My dear Archie, obviously it is. Otherwise,
how can we get at her true feeling ? Billy no
longer counts. Viola is the one to tackle. Viola
is the one to frighten. So we must get her in
here, by hook or by crook, to see us billing and
cooing. Listen ! "

Peg crept on tiptoe to the door and put one ear
to the keyhole.

" Billy is going along the passage to Viola's
room ! "

Hay made a swift, strong movement towards
the door. " Good God ! " he cried.

" Where are you going ? "

" Out. Out. Quick ! "

Peg barred the way. " No, you don't ! " she said.

" Sssh ! I can hear Billy speaking."

Hay heard Billy speaking also. There came a
loud rapping on the door.

" Open the door ! " shouted Billy.

" Hurrah ! " whispered Peg. " Now who says
I'm over-confident."

" Open the door ; do you hear ? "

." Stand quite still, Archie, and do nothing.

When I give the word, open the door." She ran excitedly to a chest and pulled open the top drawer.

Hay gazed at her. " What are you going to do ? " he asked.

" Stage-manage the scene."

Laughing softly, she drew out a Japanese kimono, got into it quickly, stepped out of her shoes, and got into bedroom slippers, little red-coloured things with low heels, ran to Hay's chair, pushed it into position, side by side with her own, and sat down.

" How does that look ? " she asked. " Wait a minute. Hark at Billy ; only hark ! Oh, it's too splendid ! "

" What am I to do ? " asked Hay, catching her excitement.

Billy hammered at the door and shouted.

" Come and sit here." Peg indicated the other chair. Hay did as he was bid.

" Now," whispered Peg, " try and look as if you loved me, and I'll do the best I can."

" But how will he get in to see us if I don't open the door ? "

" Through the dressing-room, of course. Both those doors are unlocked. He'll discover that quick enough. For goodness sake look love-sick. At present you only look bored."

"What an awful game this is," groaned Hay.

"It is, it is. But be brave, be plucky. We're winning all along the line!"

She put her head upon his shoulder and smiled sweetly.

CHAPTER XVI

BILLY flung open the dressing-room door. He was in a white heat of rage.

"Oh, Billy!" said Peg, in a voice of gentle reproof.

Billy glared at Hay. "Get out of my room," he cried.

Hay turned round slowly. "Are you talking to me?" he asked.

"My dear William," added Peg, "you mustn't break into other people's rooms in this way, you know."

Billy struck a melodramatic attitude. It was not effective. It was not dignified. It was, indeed, rather funny, because his whole appearance was so agreeably ordinary, so untheatrical.

"I have nothing to say to you," he said, eyeing his wife sternly. "Your conduct has been so disgraceful that I shall never speak to you again. My business is with this—gentleman."

He made his pause in the conventional place. He hissed the word gentleman in the conventional way. It is wonderful how technically correct according to the conventions of the stage all men are when deeply moved who have never been on the stage. Equally unconsciously Hay became theatrical, although quietly so.

" I shall be glad to give you an appointment in the morning," he said coldly. " I am engaged just now."

" Any time after eleven to-morrow," put in Peg brightly. " Good night."

Billy marched into the room slowly. His face was white with anger. He struggled bravely to maintain his self-control and dignity. He halted some yards away from Archie's chair. For a moment he said nothing.

" Dear old Billy," thought Peg, " how funny he does look ! "

He did look funny, but it was not kind to think so. He was so obviously labouring under intense emotion. He spoke as quietly as he could. " I have known you," he said, addressing Hay, " gettin' on for twenty years."

" Twenty-five, I think, William," said Peg.

" Twenty-five and three months, to be correct," said Hay.

" But," continued Billy, ignoring the interruption, " if anyone had told me that you were this kind of fellow I'd have knocked him down."

" What kind of fellow ? " asked Hay.

Billy's voice became thick. " The kind of fellow who ruins a friend's home and happiness by taking away his wife."

Peg could not resist it. " The wife likes it," she said.

" You—shock me ! " said Billy.

Hay was unable to refrain from a touch of anger. " It would interest me to know what you call a man who ruins a friend's home and happiness by flirting with his wife."

" I call him," shouted Billy, " what every decent-minded man calls him—a low, detestable blackguard."

Hay looked straightly at his friend. " That's precisely what *I* call him," he said.

" Low, detestable blackguards are the most charming kind of men," said Peg.

Ignoring his wife entirely, Billy made a movement towards Hay. " And yet that is what you deliberately have done."

All he got from Hay was a short " indeed."

" My dear William, don't put it in that crude way. This is love."

" Not content with ruining my house, you have smashed up the perfect happiness—the perfect relationship that existed between my wife and myself, and driven her into the most dreadful path a woman can enter."

Peg laughed softly. " I never heard a very broad shoulder called a dreadful path before, William."

" I must ask you to be quiet," cried Billy.

" You might just as well ask a leopard to change his spots," returned Peg, her spirits rising higher and higher.

Hay spoke scornfully. " Have you nearly finished ? " he asked.

" No, I've not," said Billy.

" When Billy begins nothing ever stops him except sleep."

Throwing a look of almost whimsical reproach at his wife, Billy turned to Hay again. " You had the impudence to suggest that we should connive in this arrangement."

"Well," said Peg, "we're not going to give you away."

"*We* have done nothing—nothing that all the world might not know ! "

Hay sprang to his feet. He could keep up the pretence no longer. "You beastly humbug," he cried.

Billy was greatly surprised. His voice took on a shrill note. "What do you mean ? . . . I merely kissed your wife in—in an airy, cousinly way, just to comfort her while you were undermining my wife's love for me. That's all."

"That's all, is it ? " said Hay. "You're one of those honourable men who kisses his friend's wife in order to oblige her husband. Your sense of honour is so nice that you clasp her passionately in your arms in a spirit of martyrdom. Your honour is so keen, and your faithfulness to your own wife is so great, that when you declare your love to another woman it is merely in an airy, cousinly way ? "

"I've told you so," replied Billy. "Good Lord, you don't think I meant anything, do you ? I often say harmless, pleasant things to women . . . don't I, Peg ? "

"Dear me, do you ? " asked Peg dryly.

" You know I do," said Billy reproachfully, all his bombast leaking out. " Dash it, you can't say that I've done anything. It was just a very ordinary flirtation, that's all. It meant nothing to me."

Hay caught him up instantly. He made no attempt to hide the tremor that shook his voice.

" No, it meant nothing to you. You merely passed the time. But I am a miserable wretch cursed with jealousy. And this flirtation of yours—which meant nothing to you—this airy, cousinly behaviour of yours, indulged in in order to pass the time, was sending the blood to my head, making the sun black, and filling my brain with suspicions that drove me nearly mad."

An expression of intense relief came into Billy's eyes. He shook himself like a great retriever, and passed his hand over his hair and cleared his throat. He even became apologetic in his attitude towards Hay, and seemed to be on the point of saying something humble.

Peg read all this. But she did not intend that her husband should get off so lightly. She intended to tease him further.

" Until you loved me, Archie," she said, " and that altered everything."

This remark gave Billy another chance. He was glad that he hadn't apologised. "Well," he said, "there is no need for Hay to worry himself. He won't have Viola on his hands much longer, believe me."

There was a nasty note of triumph in his voice that the others were quick to catch.

"What do you mean? " asked Hay.

"She has been trying to persuade me all day that these goings on of yours were all spoof. I didn't believe so. She doesn't believe so now, and she's only got one idea in this world."

"Only one! How economical," said Peg, trying to hide a returning uneasiness under a continued tone of badinage. "She'll be able to make a hobby of it."

Billy touched his tie. He was now normal again. He felt that he had a trump card still in his hand. Peg should see whether it was wise to try and make him look a fool! By Jove she should.

"At this moment," he continued, "she is packing her things to catch the first possible train to town to-morrow with me."

"Why? " demanded Archie.

Billy flung out his hands. "Why? " he asked generally. "He asks me why! "

" I ask you why too, dear William," said Peg.

Her chaffing tone annoyed him horribly.
" Now then," he thought ; " now then."

" To bring an action for divorce against Archibald Hay, that's all."

He swung round, marched into the dressing-room, slammed both its doors behind him, and went downstairs noisily.

" Who looks the fool now ? " he asked himself.

For a moment Peg and Archie both looked fools. They watched the door out of which Billy had passed incredulously. Then they looked at each other. They were aghast, wordless.

Peg was the first to find her voice. " Good heavens ! " she exclaimed. " She could too ! "

The same appalling thought had come to Hay. His declaration in the hall that morning, his subsequent disappearance with Peg—watched, no doubt, by Meakin, Stanner, and the others—the scene below after dinner, the two hours that he had spent locked in Peg's bedroom, also, no doubt, taken note of by Meakin, Stanner, and the others !

He lost his head. He forgot his inherited ideas of chivalry and respect. " Now do you see what this great scheme of yours has brought us all to with your marvellous sense of humour ? No wonder she's furious. No wonder she means to be revenged. I wish I'd been shot before I was mad enough to take part in this hare-brained plan!"

"I don't believe it," gasped Peg. "Billy's romancing. She couldn't do it."

"She going to do it. And she has the right."

"I don't believe it. It isn't true." Peg's voice rang out piercingly. "She is no more willing to make a horrible scandal than we were. It isn't true."

She ran to the door, fumbled with trembling fingers with the key, and turned it.

"It isn't true, it isn't true!" she repeated pitifully. She opened the door, went out slowly, looked along the passage, and came back swiftly. All the colour had left her face. "It *is* true!" she said. "The passage is filled with her luggage."

CHAPTER XVII

It was true enough, all too true. Viola, with Stanner's wondering aid, had already packed two large dress-trunks, and was working feverishly upon a third.

She and Stanner hurried about in a room littered with frocks, chiffons, hats, shoes, and all

the things that are necessary to the well-being of
a woman. Tissue-paper was strewn everywhere,
upon the floor, upon the bed; it gaped out of
empty hat-boxes, lapped out of empty drawers,
crinkled uneasily in the swish of Viola's dress.
It had been Viola's intention to spend a week at
Brighton with Peg as soon as the men had settled
down in the cottage. She had in consequence
brought with her from London far more things
than she needed for a mere golf holiday.

She had been rapping out quick, sharp orders
to Stanner. This young woman's inexperience
had not been rendered any the less annoying by
her uneasiness. On the contrary, her suspicion
that matters had reached a crisis, together with
her inexpertness in such delicate work as the folding of dresses, had made her a greater hindrance
than help.

So Viola had done most of the packing herself.
Her rage and chagrin had a curious effect upon
her. It caused her to take a sort of angry pleasure in folding and packing her things with the
greatest care and precision. She set herself
deliberately to work. She made Stanner unhang
one dress at a time. This she spread upon the
bed. Between each careful fold she placed a

sheet of tissue-paper. When ready, she handed the curious-looking thing to Stanner to lower gently into the trunk. With dress after dress she pursued the same expert tactics, until the two cases which Peg had seen in the passage were placed there to give her more space in her room.

Hat after hat, all large and befeathered, were removed from the wardrobe, and treated with quick, deft fingers. A piece of tissue-paper here, a sheet there, and into its box it went.

And all the time Viola's brains were at work as quickly as were her fingers. Yes, revenge. That was the only thing to satisfy. To make Peg and Archie suffer because they were making her suffer. To make them pay for their deceit, their long series of double-faced doings, their hidden understandings.

At the moment her whole mind was concentrated on this furious desire to hurt these two. The pain and grief that she would feel eventually at Archie's desertion were at present swamped by the stinging of her wounded vanity. The fact that Archie could have lived with her while loving another woman so damaged her self-esteem, so smashed her sense of dignity, that she could hardly trust herself to think about it. To

have the knowledge that she had been living in
a fool's paradise suddenly forced upon her in such
a way was almost more than she could bear. She
lashed herself into a fury when she realised how
pitiful she must have appeared to Billy in her
struggle to win expressions of love from a man
whose love belonged to someone else. All the
turbulence of her somewhat Southern temperament was stirred up at the bare thought of having
made a laughing-stock of herself. It put her
into a frenzy of self-disgust, a frenzy so painful
as to make it necessary for someone to pay for
it. All the best of her nature, her love and her
faith, were carried away in the torrent of her
rage. Utterly careless of appearances, and of
the feelings of others, she allowed herself to be
swept and whirled into the maelstrom of un-
restrained anger.

With a sort of fierce joy she built up a picture
of the discomfort to which she could put, not
only Archie and Peg, but Billy as well. Archie
would not be the only one to undergo the horrors
of newspaper comment—a thing he dreaded and
abhorred. Peg, Peg would be dragged into dis-
gusting publicity as well—Peg more than Archie.

The story of her behaviour in the cottage would be gloated over by potmen and bus-drivers, housemaids and men-servants, would be the topic of conversation among all her friends, the subject for facetious headlines in the papers, and announcements on the bills that would suddenly stare at passers-by in the streets and gleam on the boards of little shops in narrow byways.

Peg, Archie, and Billy—the three people who knew how great a fool she had made of herself—would all be punished at once. She could devise no better, no riper means of punishment than by throwing the history of this one May day into the public's maw.

In this mood Viola was a very dangerous woman. A rather indolent, slow-moving woman generally, who liked things to run very smoothly and quietly, who never fetched anything herself or did anything for herself if there was someone by to fetch or do it for her, who did not, as a rule, permit the true state of her feelings to be seen, there was no personal trouble to which she would not go once she was fairly roused. Only once before in her life had she been so terribly and completely roused. When she was sixteen, a tall, slight, graceful girl, sailing through her days with

a sort of regal graciousness, always with a slightly
tilted chin and slightly raised eyebrows, always
with certain things to do at certain times—her
horse at ten o'clock, a chat with her mother for
an hour before luncheon, her book alone in her
room till tea, a letter or two to write before
dinner, always the same amount of time in which
to dress for dinner—she had gone with Peg and
other schoolfellows who were her guests at her
father's house to a fancy-dress ball. This was a
yearly Christmas affair given by one of the hunting women of the county—a Duke's daughter, a
loud, vulgar, self-indulgent creature—quite one
of the things to do. The young people's ball
followed the ball to which the grown-up portion
of the county made a point of going. One was
held on Twelfth Night and the other on the thir-
teenth. Viola had gone as Pierrot, after the
painting of Comerre, and Peg as Pierrette. They
made a very charming picture together—Viola
tall, slim, arrogant, her large eyes very luminous
under the tight-fitting black cap, in a perfectly
white face with red lips ; Peg all smiles and
dimples, bubbling over with fun, a little rogue
in porcelain. The men of the house-party came
in to see how the children were going on, and

Lady Mary's husband—a bull-necked, tubby person, whose way it was to touch people when he spoke to them, either laying a hand on an arm, holding the button of a coat, tapping a chest to drive home his long-ago discovered inspirations on matters of importance—was greatly attracted by Viola. "Corkin'" he called her, and he danced with her twice. Although Viola considered him to be a most objectionable little cad, he was the host, and it appealed to her vanity to be the only girl in the room to dance with him. Winchmore was as much amused by Viola's quiet patronage and stiff-necked tolerance as he was stirred by her beauty of face and form. He invariably kissed young girls when they were pretty—openly, of course, why not? He had daughters of his own, dear little things. In his usual way he halted under the mistletoe, put his arm round Viola, and bent forward to kiss her. He found not only that she became like a steel rod to his touch, but that two strong fists were held fiercely against his chest. He guffawed. This was immense. Hoighty-toighty, what a little queen! He would have it, however hard the struggle. He called to a friend. "What's the bettin'!" he laughed. "Do I storm this

castle or not ? " Viola gave a twist to free herself. Winchmore put his other arm round her,
and drew her to him. He never had seen such
fury in any eyes. Viola, using all her strength to
get away, managed to say, " If you do, I'll make
you pay ! " He roared. " Oh, drop it," said
his friend. " The child don't like it." . . .
" Like it be damned," said Winchmore. " She's
got to like it," and he bent suddenly forward
and kissed her on the lips. Then he let her go.
Viola, with her white satin things all creased and
crumpled, her sugar-cone hat lying at her feet,
breathing hard, looked the man over, for a
moment, with eyes that were hot with rage. Her
nostrils were distended like those of a thorough-
bred that had been flogged with the whip. Her
lips were pressed together tightly. Her whole
young body shook with passionate anger. Winchmore rather wished that he had not persisted.
He thought that he caught a look of calculating
venomosity in those two gleaming eyes. He
was right.

From the moment that Viola picked up her
Pierrot hat and slipped back into the crowd only
one desire possessed her—to be even with that
man. She nursed this desire in silence for a

month. A hundred schemes took shape in her mind. She would bring ridicule upon him by going to the meet and slashing him across the face with her crop. She would wait until he came round with the plate at the morning service —he performed all these kinds of duties with much elbow—and calmly place a bottle of beer into it. She would do anything, anything, to make him publicly foolish. Her chance came early in February. Major and Lady Mary Winchmore got up yearly theatricals at the Town Hall in aid of the funds of the Parish Nurses. It was a fashionable event. Viola's father, Canon Pilkington, was down with the gout, so she took her mother. Winchmore was not taking part in the performance on the stage, but was largely in evidence in the foyer, and here, there, and everywhere. It was the first time that he and Viola had met since the dance. At the end of the performance, when Tubby was receiving the congratulations of the County and was the centre of a group of hunting people, men and women of his particular set, she deliberately went forward, dropped a shilling into his outstretched hand, and said very quietly, " Call Mrs. Pilkington's carriage, please."

She did this when she was a child, a slip of a girl. Her vanity had been wounded, she had been made to look ridiculous, and so she intended to be revenged, and never rested until she was revenged. She was now a woman of twenty-seven. She was in the full glory of her beauty, and knew it. She never had played the queen with Archie. He was the only living person who had won all her love, whom she had followed with a curious humbleness, to whose ways and habits she had regulated her own, so far as it was possible. Archie was well enough known, a striking enough personality. His athleticism had made the name of Hay familiar to many who had never seen the man. But—she knew this, and it was not unpleasing—he had been called Mrs. Hay's husband for years. She had loved him so whole-heartedly that she had been content to be with him during the best time of the year in such far from civilised places as the one she was in at the moment. She had willingly foregone the pleasures and excitement of several London seasons to go into the country with him on cricket tours and golf tours, and had buried herself with all her exquisite clothes in places where it did not matter how she dressed or who saw her. Of the general admiration which had been the breath of her life before marriage during her meteor-like course in society she wanted nothing. Archie had been her life. Archie had been her kingdom, her king, her god. She had served him, she that had never served. She had pandered to him, considered him, she that had pandered to and considered no one but herself. And when at last, hipped and hurt at what she naturally considered to be callous treatment, she had made an effort at revolt, she had discovered that all her service and consideration and adoration had been laid at the feet of an indifferent god, no, not an indifferent god, but a god whose love had been given to another woman.

Therefore, revenge! She told herself, as she packed her things, that the best revenge was to make Archie's treachery public, just as she told herself, years before, that the way to get her own back from Winchmore was to make him a public laughing-stock. However much it hurt her to be aware that, as a matter of fact, great as her desire was to punish Archie, her desire to punish Peg was even greater. For Peg had known— she knew everything, she was so quick—something of Viola's grievance. She had guessed, although she had not said anything, that Viola was dissatisfied, disturbed, discontented. Who could imagine that Peg could continue to care about a man like Billy when there was such a man as Archie in the world, in her almost daily life, alone with her frequently ? It was obvious that she had taken advantage of Archie's waning affection for herself—Viola—to creep into his heart. It was treachery of an indescribable nature. It cried for punishment. And it should be punished very fully !

CHAPTER XVIII

His duties duly and artistically performed, Meakin had changed his black clothes for a smoking-suit of brown velvet. It was a very smart affair. The coat was double-breasted, and opened widely in front. The collar, the cuffs, and the lapels of it were piped with blue silk. The trousers, very wide and somewhat peg-topped—of the Tom and Jerry period—had a piping of the same blue silk down the seams. In this wonderful confection, James Meakin settled down in the kitchen to smoke and read.

The cook had gone to bed, Stanner was with Mrs. Hay—fine woman, Mrs. Hay—so Meakin had placed the lamp on the corner of the spotless table, pulled up a deck-chair—his own property —in order that the light should fall over his left shoulder, had set a box of cigars of the same brand as Sir William's—he ran a bill for these with Sir William's man—within easy reach, and lay full stretch in the chair, upon two cushions. His book was a new volume of the recollections of a well-known man of the world, borrowed from Mudie's, to which library Meakin was an old subscriber.

He made a picture of extreme comfort, not to say luxury. The lamplight seemed to make his velvet glow. It fell softly upon his intelligent, well-cut, well-shaved face and black, smooth hair with its accurate parting. It showed up his brown silk socks, and settled with a white patch upon his black shiny shoes.

The kitchen was a pleasant, airy room, designed by an artistic modern hand. On each side of the big fire-place there was a long casement window with small panes of bottle-green glass. One of these windows was open, and through it could be seen a square of star-mottled sky. The clean air came in refreshingly. All the paint in the room was white, and the walls were covered with a light distemper. Upon them, here and there, hung pictures of horses taken from an illustrated paper, neatly tacked up by Meakin. The dresser, with its prim array of plates, was not unpicturesque. A large bowl of primroses sat upon the table. Everything was in apple-pie order.

Meakin was not satisfied, however. Throwing his eyes round on a sort of inspection, he caught sight of a pair of the cook's out-of-door shoes— large, ungainly things, with heels much trodden down. They annoyed him excessively. He wished that he had seen them before arranging himself. He would have hidden them. As it was, he held the volume up so that his view of the offending things might be blocked. But he was unable to settle down. The shoes rankled. He felt that they made a jarring note in the room. He threw out a sigh, got out of the chair slowly, and with the air of a man who is a martyr to a good cause, picked up the shoes, deposited them in a drawer in the dresser, and returned to his chair, his book, and his cigar.

Presently he shut the book and laid it respectfully upon the table. He found it impossible to concentrate his attention upon the good stories, which mostly related to dukes, cabinet ministers, sporting peers, and beautiful women of title—

the only people who interested him. He found himself lying back, puffing quietly at his cigar, with his eyes on the ceiling. A smile played round his mouth. As he had told Stanner just before Mrs. Hay's bell had summoned her up to the bedroom, he was up to date with the state of the game. In the passage outside the kitchen door there was a very useful square hole in the wall opening into the hall. This had been constructed by the architect for the purpose of passing plates, hot vegetables, and other things into the hall from the cook to the domestics on duty at meal times. When not in use this hole was shuttered up at both ends, but by keeping the passage end open, and by placing a lead pencil under the other shutter, Meakin, seated comfortably in the passage, was able to hear all the conversation that took place in the hall, except when it was conducted in quiet tones.

Meakin had never left that hole from the moment that Sir William had returned except once, and that was when he had entered the hall to inform Sir William, at what he took to be the most dramatically correct moment, that his bed was ready at the " Cat and Fiddle." He had therefore heard everything—the quiet triumph of Lady Hutton and the Major, the subsequent attempt on the Major's part to "be nice" to Sir William, the sudden panic of the Major at Mrs. Hay's brilliant treatment of Sir William, the comic horror of Sir William and the statement by Mrs. Hay which put a new complexion on the whole affair, the love-making of Lady Hutton and the Major, the withdrawal of Lady Hutton, as Meakin considered badly beat, the ragging of the Major by Sir William—Meakin had the greatest difficulty to prevent himself from choking with suppressed laughter—the rough-and-tumble, the fright of Lady Hutton and Mrs. Hay, the most effective exit of Lady Hutton and the Major, and finally the raging, frenzied outburst of Mrs. Hay, to which Meakin had listened open-mouthed.

He congratulated himself upon having been highly entertained. He could not remember ever to have spent so enjoyable a day, one fuller of surprises. He sympathised with Mrs. Hay. She was undoubtedly a fine woman. She had a right to demand more of the Major's time and considerably more of his attention. He had thought that she possessed underneath her languid, graceful manner a pretty hot temper, but he had never dreamed her capable of such a pyrotechnical display as he had witnessed.

His admiration of Lady Hutton remained as great as ever. He always had regarded her management of Sir William as not very far short of perfection. Her plan to stop the flirtation between Mrs. Hay and Sir William was, to his way of thinking, a stroke of genius, quite surprisingly well carried out in the morning by the Major. She had said many things during the day that took his fancy, and her invention of the bedroom plan stirred him to real enthusiasm. He considered the Major had come out amazingly well. He had not given him the credit of possessing such sterling histrionic ability. If he had not been sent into the Army he might have been a distinguished man.

In regard to his master Meakin had no difficulty in making up his mind. Sir William had behaved exactly as he would have prophesied. All the same his affection for his master remained undisturbed. He had many good points. Having summed up the position so far as the performers were concerned, Meakin lit a second cigar and turned his mind to the position as it was likely to affect the future.

He chuckled at the complete somersault that events had taken. In the morning divorce had been spoken of by the Major—Mrs. Hay and Sir William had then been the culprits. Now it was Mrs. Hay who spoke of divorce, and the Major and Lady Hutton were the parties concerned. Of one thing he felt certain. Mrs. Hay would carry out her threat. Mrs. Hay would never rest until she had made havoc of the lives of all concerned.

Well he, Meakin, had no squeamish notions as to divorce. It was true that it had been taken up by suburban people, but it had been originated more or less by a king and practised largely by the aristocracy. If he and Stanner chose to say in court exactly what had happened in the cottage during the course of that adventurous day Mrs. Hay would win. No judge would believe that a man like the Major would spend two hours in a beautiful woman's room in order to bring about a reconciliation between himself and his wife. No, no. Judges acted on stereotyped lines in regard to human nature. They would hold that to put forward a plea at playing at adultery was contempt of court. Such a plea would inevitably prejudice the judge against the Major, and the judge would take good care that his prejudice was shared by the jury.

Whether Meakin would give, or allow Stanner to give, evidence as to the bedroom episode depended, of course, on what orders he received from Sir William. He was there to carry out orders. He thought it very likely that Sir William, recognising that he had made a bit of an ass of himself, would let things take their course. It would give him the only chance he had of being top-dog with Lady Hutton, of playing the grandly magnanimous part of forgiving his wife and taking her back. However things might eventually shape, the fact remained that the whole episode had served to make Meakin a trifle less dissatisfied with the golf cottage, to forget the fact that he was losing the pleasures of a London season and his evenings at the club, at the theatres, the music-halls, and the exhibition.

At this point of his reflections, and just as he was about to take up his book again and mix in the society of the only people who, to his mind, had any right to live, he heard his name called by Sir William.

He raised his eyebrows and remained in his

chair. Technically speaking, he was, at this hour of the day, no longer Meakin the gentleman's gentleman. He was Mr. James Meakin, gentleman. Any service that he might perform after he had dressed Sir William Hutton for dinner he regarded in the light of a favour. Since he had been at the cottage he had been in bed and asleep at this hour. He hoped that Sir William would imagine, when he received no answer, that he was in bed now.

So he gave no answer. Nor did he alter his attitude by the fraction of an inch. Sir William did not raise his voice again, but in a moment or two came into the kitchen passage, stopped, presumably saw the light under the door, and marched forward sharply.

Meakin regarded such a proceeding as most undignified and unwarrantable. As a servant he was technically non-existent. He made no attempt at subterfuge. He continued to read and smoke quietly.

Billy threw open the kitchen door. " Oh, you are here ! " he said.

Meakin gathered himself together and rose. His eyebrows were slightly raised. " Yes, Sir William," he replied.

"Well then, why the devil didn't you come when you were called?"

Billy's eyes fell on his man's clothes. "Good Lord," he thought, "velvet piped with blue—brown silk socks and shoes by Bumble! Well, of all the . . ."

But he made a mental note of the entire get-up. He decided instantly that his order should be for blue velvet, piped with brown silk, blue silk socks.

"Can I do anything for you, Sir William?" asked Meakin, with respect, but with some slight condescension.

"Yes, you can. Come with me."

CHAPTER XIX

MEAKIN followed Sir William Hutton into the hall. He was not going to call his master's attention to a distinct breach of contract. He decided to make allowance for what was a very exciting period in the lives of them all. A natural curiosity—or, as Meakin would have called it, a natural interest—may have had something to do with his decision. He looked to see which piece of Doulton ware it was that Sir

William had flung into the grate. He was glad that it was the nicest piece. He liked everything to be done well. He saw from a quick glance at the whisky-bottle, newly opened that night, that Sir William must have had at least three pegs. He bent down and picked up a small tortoise-shell comb that lay on one of the rugs. The other rug he straightened with his toe.

Billy led the way upstairs.

Stanner, who was pulling a trunk out on to the passage, threw a piteous glance at Meakin. It was answered by a prolonged wink.

Billy entered his dressing-room. "Wait here, will you," he said.

"Very good, Sir William," said Meakin.

Billy knocked at the bedroom door.

"Come in," said Hay.

Billy went in. Meakin took the opportunity of looking in. He saw the Major standing erect in the middle of the room. He could see nothing of Lady Hutton.

"I'm sorry to bother," said Billy.

"No bother," said Hay.

"I forgot to say—at least I don't remember havin' said—that Viola made me promise to take her to London to-morrow. She'll be leavin' so abominably early that there'll be no time to pack in the mornin', so I think I'd better pack now."

" I see," said Hay. " Please do."

" Of course," said Peg.

" Yes, but dash it, *I* can't pack. *You* know that," said Billy.

" Yes," replied Peg. " I've always seen to that when Meakin has been away ; haven't I ? "

" Yes, and jolly well, too. You're a corkin' good packer."

" Thank you, William," said Peg faintly.

There was a silence.

Meakin edged nearer the dressing-room door. He could just catch a glimpse of Lady Hutton. She was sitting limply in an upright chair. Her face looked very white against the crimson of her kimono, and her eyes very wide and tired. Her hands were folded in her lap, and one small foot in its red shoe rested wearily upon the other.

" My London clothes are all in here," said Billy. " There was no room in that box of a dressin'-room. . . . Would you mind Meakin comin' in ? "

" Why the dickens should we mind ? " asked Hay irritably.

" Of course not," said Peg.

" Thanks," said Billy.

He turned. " Meakin," he called.

" Sir William ? " Meakin appeared at the door.

Hay threw an astonished contemptuous glance at the brown velvet clothes. Peg was accustomed to Meakin's idiosyncrasies.

" Oh, come in, do," snapped Billy. " Don't stand there lookin' like livin' statuary. Pull out the trouser-case."

He indicated a long leather case that was under the dressing-table. It was constructed to carry a dozen pairs of trousers at full stretch.

Meakin did so.

" In there quick," said Billy. " Don't try and show us that you're an artist. Just pitch 'em in."

" Pitch 'em, sir," murmured Meakin, with a slight shudder.

He opened the trunk and blew into it carefully. Then he went to the wardrobe that stood nearest to the dressing-room door. A number of coats hung from brass rods on shoulder-pieces. A dozen pairs of trousers lay one upon the other on a shelf.

Archie and Peg seemed to welcome this interlude. The prosaic note of the proceedings came as a relief into an atmosphere that was charged with emotion. Only Peg knew what had happened after she had made the discovery of Viola's luggage in the passage. She had not supposed that Archie ever could have lost his self-control so completely. He had said things to her that she had already forgiven but would never forget. She told herself, as she sat limp and tired, watching Meakin transferring Billy's clothes from one place to another, that she had not known until that night several of the things that she thought she had known very well. She began to feel surprised at the way trouble had acted upon herself. She had not supposed herself capable of a display of hysteria under any circumstances, nor did she know how wholly necessary Billy was to her with all his faults. She thought that she had known old Billy through and through. She had been mistaken. She had not dreamed that it was possible for him to side with anyone, even a fascinating and clever woman, against his oldest friend, as he had proved that he had done. She had known that Archie loved his wife, but not how very much he loved her. She also had known that in

Viola vanity formed three-quarters of her character, and that she was capable of an overmastering desire for revenge. But she had not supposed that even Viola, in so many respects a charming woman and in every respect a good woman in the ordinary meaning of the word, could carry her desire to hurt those who had hurt her so far as she intended to carry it at the moment.

She saw for the first time how very curiously trouble acts on people who are for the most part extraordinarily free from trouble, so far as it affects them personally. She felt about herself, Archie, Viola, and Billy much as a man feels about a party of intimate friends after he has seen how they behaved in a shipwreck or a train accident or a fire, that she and they possessed characteristics of which no one had known anything.

She brought herself up, finally, face to face with the existing condition of affairs. With a quickening of the pulse, she could not help confessing that she and Archie, Viola and Billy were in a very much worse tangle after all her work than they had been in before she had taken things in her hands. If Archie had been the one to consider that he had been injured, he could have been dealt with diplomatically. If Billy had been the one with the grievance, all would have been easy. But Viola was the one, Viola, who as a girl had never rested until revenge had healed her wounded vanity. Everything, therefore, remained to be done in order to restore peace and happiness to the golf cottage, everything.

Billy saw that Meakin, having an audience, was giving a demonstration of how clothes should be packed. It was too much for his nerves. He snatched up a pair of trousers. "Catch hold," he said, and flung them at the man.

"Thank you, Sir William." Meakin held them under his chin and spread the legs out. His expression was that of a man who performs a delicate operation, requiring great accuracy and a lifelong training.

"Oh, curse the creases," snapped Billy.

"I generally iron them, Sir William," replied Meakin.

"Bustle up, please."

Meakin was not going to bustle, either for the trousers' sake or his own. There was only one way to pack trousers. He did not intend, on or off duty, to look undignified. With infinite and

painstaking care he went to work, ignoring his
master's agonised glances completely. Not
happy at having put each leg crease to crease, he
laid the trousers out flat upon the lid of the case,
stroked them tenderly, pulled them gently, and
then, with an air of slight agitation, put one leg
right back and looked to see that the other was
in order. When completely satisfied, the other
leg returned to its place, and was again stroked
before both legs were placed softly into the case.

These proceedings nearly maddened Billy.
" Oh, ram 'em in, will you ? " he said, tapping
his foot.

Meakin looked up. " If I could do this, Sir
William," he suggested, " in the early hours of
the morning . . ."

Billy threw another pair at him. " Get on ! "
he growled.

" Very good, Sir William."

The operation was repeated. Meakin was
not pursuing these tactics in order to annoy his
master, or because he was angry at having been
called from his few hours of leisure. He was
honestly free from all ulterior motives. He was
the conscientious man. He was the artist. He
was the workman. It was impossible for him

to scamp. If the house had suddenly burst into flames he would have continued in the same thorough way. His grandfather and his father had treated clothes as though they were a religion. It was part of his nature, it was in his blood to do so also. When other youths had been devoting hours to cricket and football, young James Meakin had been taking lessons in the arts of packing, ironing, folding, and brushing.

At first the slowness irritated Hay almost as much as it irritated Billy. He wanted nothing so much as to get rid of Billy and Meakin and turn to Peg for advice. Was he to go out and appeal to Viola, or would Peg prefer to do so— that was what had to be settled, and settled as soon as possible. But presently Meakin's utter devotion to his business began to please him. He thought that it was good. A thing to praise, not blame. He himself had not bothered about a man since he had left the Service. They were more nuisance than they were worth. He hated to have his things pawed about and fussed over as though they belonged to a woman or a dressy brute. He just dressed, according to the weather and orthodoxy. When he packed he simply filled up his cases. Coats and trousers and the rest

went in. All his attention was paid either to
his guns, rods, or clubs. All the same he admired
Meakin. It was the right spirit. It showed
training, discipline, and *esprit de corps*.

The same feeling presently seemed to pervade
Billy and Peg as well, for although they were in
the same, or much the same, chaotic state of
mind as Archie was, they too settled into watch-
ful silence. Meakin's quiet dignity and scrupulous
regard to the decisions of conscience seemed to
act as a sedative. They watched him as villagers
watch the shoeing of a horse, or passers-by the
laying down of steaming asphalte—with gloomy
concentration.

In the next room Viola was tying up the last
of her hat-boxes, and in a little room at the end
of the corridor Stanner was saying her prayers
while she endeavoured to imagine what would
happen next.

CHAPTER XX

" Now," said Hay, when he and Peg had the
room to themselves again. " We have to face
facts."

" Yes," said Peg, " yes. . . . Well ? "

" We must go straight out and make them

discuss this matter fully. We must tell them precisely what we've done and why we did it. Do you agree?"

Peg pulled herself together. She rose, went over to her dressing-table, opened one of the small drawers, selected a clean handkerchief and held it under a bottle of sweet-pea scent while she tilted it on its head twice. She never could take any definite step without a clean handkerchief properly scented. Then she turned towards the expectant Hay.

"No," she said.

"Why not?"

"What has to be done must be done by me," she replied. "This latest trouble has been caused by me."

"No, no," said Hay, anxious to make up to Peg, if possible, for his recent outburst of blame. "It was an easier thing to talk of than to do. We have acted too realistically, that's all. Nothing can be lost now by the truth from all sides. . . . If I lose Viola, I lose everything."

"You shall not lose her, Archie. Send her to me, here."

Hay was greatly relieved. He protested weakly, however. "I think that you've done enough. I don't mean to let you do any more of my work. Let me go to Viola."

Peg was determined. "You've never heard any of the things that Viola says in temper," she said. "I have, and if I don't take the edge off before you two meet you'll never be able to live together again as long as you're alive."

"Why should you face it?" he asked.

"Because," said Peg, "I know Viola, and you don't, and because I set out to put things right this morning, and I can't rest until I've done so. It's very late, dear man," she added, with a wan smile. "So don't argue."

"Very well," said Hay. "Have it your own way for the second time. But do it at once. Honestly, I can't stand much more of this. I feel at the end of my tether."

"I am ready for her now."

"How am I to get her into this room?"

"Tell her that she is on no account to come in."

Hay looked sharply at Peg. Her remark was the most extraordinary one that he had ever heard.

"Tell her that she is on no account . . ."

"Please."

It was an order. Peg was in command. It was not for him to question the wisdom or the sense of an order. It was his duty to carry it out. He turned on his heels, marched to the door, unlocked it, opened it, and left the room.

Peg heard Hay call " Viola " once and then again. He had a good voice. The name sounded well.

She heard Viola reply, " I have nothing to say to you, Major Hay."

Hay's next remark came clearly. " There are one or two things I should like to say to you."

" I am afraid they will not interest me. I shall be glad if you will allow me to pass."

Viola was then in the corridor.

" I beg your pardon," said Hay.

Peg heard the sound of footsteps.

" Thank you," said Viola.

" I must ask you not to go into Peg's room," came from Hay hastily.

" Pray don't trouble yourself. Wild horses couldn't drag me there."

Peg smiled.

Hay spoke again. " Peg particularly asked me not to allow you to go in."

" Really ! "

There was an angry movement, and a hurried one. " I'll shut the door, please."

" I'll shut the door, thank you."

The door was shut. But when Peg looked up, suddenly conscious that she was not alone, she saw Viola standing in the room, eyeing her venomously.

CHAPTER XXI

VIOLA'S face was very white, and her eyes very wide and luminous. She still wore the white dress in which she had come down for dinner. She stood close against the door, with one hand behind her on the handle. She held her chin high, and her bosom rose and fell quickly.

Half closing her eyes as she looked at her, Peg could see a young, slim, indignant Pierrot, all in white and white of face, breathing heavily, with her lips pressed tightly. She suddenly remembered all the details of that other scene at the fancy-dress ball and what had happened to Major Winchmore. There was to be another Major Winchmore, then ? Peg intuitively recognised that she stood for that man in this quarrel, not Archie.

That was good.

" I thought you would come," she said.

" You were right."

" I am glad you have come."

" You'll be sorry before I leave you."

" I hope not."

" I can assure you that you will."

" Then why have you come ? "

" To give you my opinion of your conduct before I go away."

" Oh, you're going away ? "

" To-morrow."

" What is your idea in going ? "

" To make you pay."

" I see."

" Yes, to make you pay. To ruin you, Margaret Hutton."

The quiet rally of question and answer was brought to an end by this vehement outcry. Up to that moment Viola's tone had been studiously quiet, although all her words came clearly and cuttingly. Then she bent forward and spoke with a bitterness of emphasis which took Peg's breath away.

There was no longer any doubt in Peg's mind as to the reason for Viola's longing for revenge. It sprang entirely from a desire to be even with the woman who had, she supposed, crept into her husband's heart. There was no wish to hurt

Archie for having taken the woman in. In a way Peg sympathised with this point of view. If the positions had been reversed, she would not have desired to punish Billy for desertion, but the woman who had attracted him. She made up her mind quickly to a course of action. She would first let Viola see how contemptible this almost animalish craving for revenge made her seem. Then she would show her why she and Archie had left the hall for the bedroom, and finally draw a true and simple picture of the manner in which Viola had made Archie suffer by her flirtation with Billy. She knew that the only way to get under Viola's armour was to re-open the wound unconsciously made in her heart by Archie. She began again in the same quiet, level voice.

"Billy tells me that you have packed your things."

"Everything."

"I can't help you then?"

"No, thank you."

"Can I send a telegram to Worthing for a motor-car?"

"I have already written one out."

" Meakin shall send it as soon as the village post office is open in the morning. You will be able to catch the mid-day train."

" That is the one I have arranged to go by."

" Billy has promised to go up with you, I hear."

" He can come or not, as he chooses."

" I think he will choose not to go."

" Let him ; I don't care."

" You know the kind of solicitor to go to ? "

" Why ' kind of solicitor,' pray ? "

" A respectable solicitor won't take up this case."

" You mean it is too disgraceful."

" Oh dear no."

" Why, then ? "

" I mean that there is no evidence for a respectable solicitor to work with."

" No evidence ! " Viola burst into scoffing laughter.

" But that, of course, isn't the point, is it ? "

" I don't know what you mean ? "

" Oh, but why ? The wish to divorce Archie is not taking you to London, is it ? You don't wish to divorce Archie."

" You are very clever."

" No, it is all quite obvious. Your only idea is to make the story of this one day public property in the one way that is possible, so that *I* may be made to look ridiculous."

" And worse."

" No, it will stop at ridicule. If you thought that it would not you would devise other means of hitting me. I think I said that you don't wish to divorce Archie."

" And I think I said that you're very clever."

" However, don't let me dissuade you from what you have made up your mind to do."

" Dissuade me ! "

" Nothing can make me seem more ridiculous than I feel at present. I was only wondering whether you couldn't devise some means of hurting me without hurting Archie as well."

" I wish for no interference from you."

" I wouldn't interfere for the world. But if revenge is to be made really effective, it seems to me that it is rather weak and ingenuous to make three people look ridiculous in order that a fourth may be held up to ridicule. That's all."

" It's a free country. You may think whatever you like."

" Revenge *is* your one desire, isn't it ? "

" Yes, it is."

" Well then, go to London to-morrow now

that you have packed, by all means. But may I suggest that you think the thing out more carefully? When you revenged yourself upon Major Winchmore you showed genuine ingenuity. You made him a laughing-stock without injuring yourself in any way. It was extremely effective and you came out well."

" I can't see why you want to drag up that old affair."

" Simply because I know that you are capable of inventing a far better scheme of revenging yourself upon me than by going to the courts."

" Anyone would think that you're anxious for me to revenge myself on you."

" I am. I know that none of us will have any peace of mind until you do."

Viola made no reply to this. Peg congratulated herself upon scoring the first point.

Viola still stood with her back to the door and with one hand on its handle. She was more than ever in a gunpowder temper, only waiting to be set alight. She always had been, even in girlhood, a little nervous of Peg when she became ultra-quiet. She was nervous of her now. She could see very clearly that Peg was holding her up to contempt.

" I am not in the least ashamed of being revengeful. And I am perfectly satisfied with the revenge I have planned—all the more because everything you say proves how anxious you are not to be dragged through the courts."

" Very well," said Peg. " Then take me through the courts. Destroy the happiness of three people, ruin your own happiness, ride roughshod over all your womanly instincts, and be satisfied if you can for having been the sole cause of this unhappy day."

" I don't intend to listen to any moralising from you, believe me ! "

" Perhaps you are wise. If I gave you my opinion on your behaviour you would carry some unpleasant thoughts with you on your journey."

Peg had applied the match.

" *My* behaviour ! " cried Viola. " You preach about *my* behaviour ! *I've* destroyed the peace of mind of four people, have I ? *I've* secretly undermined the love of a man for his wife, have I ? . . . Let me tell you that I loathe myself for having lived under the same roof with you. I loathe myself for having trusted my husband under the same roof with you. Your frankness, your friendship, your healthy-mindedness are worthless. You're a

sham, a fraud. But you shall pay for it, whatever it costs me. I'll drag you through the
divorce court. I'll disgrace you in the eyes of
all your friends. All the world shall know that
you are a light woman ! "

Peg sprang to her feet. " How *dare* you say
that to me ! How dare *you* ! "

" It's the truth ! "

" You know it to be a lie. *You* of all people
to say such a thing to me."

Viola flung back her head. " You talk about
me, me, as though anything I've done could be
mentioned in the same breath with your doings ! "

" Can you deceive yourself into believing that
they can't ? "

" There is no need for deceit. I know what
you've done. Everyone in the house knows,
even the servants. . . . *I've* done nothing."

" Nothing ? You call it nothing to have been
untrue to a lifelong friendship—nothing to have
deliberately set yourself to break up the lives
of three people—nothing to have made a man
like Archie miserable and wretched ? These
things may mean nothing to you. To me they
mean everything, everything."

" Oh, what virtue ! what morality ! All this

from the woman who openly confessed her love for her friend's husband ! "

" We were pretending for a good reason. You know it. You never were deceived for a moment, until we came up here."

" Came up here and locked the door ! There can be no explanation for that, none. It was unthinkable, unthinkable ! "

Peg steadied herself. There was a wildness in Viola's last outburst that showed that she was almost on the verge of tears. Once bring the tears and the rest would be easy.

Peg's voice became grave and quiet. " There is an explanation," she said. " I believed that the best way of saving us all from much misery was to make you think that Archie and I love each other. It was the final move of the plan I arranged this morning after breakfast when Archie came back distracted, having seen you in Billy's arms. He and you are equally jealous people. He was appalled at what you had done, and what you might not be going to do. And I was frightened, not only for my own future happiness with Billy, but at the thought of the lengths to which Archie's jealousy might take him. I decided to shock you and Billy out of your flirtation by pretending to be in love with Archie. You know that I am telling you the truth. You found us out almost at once. You can't deny that?"

"I don't deny it. I did think that you were pretending, and I thought I knew why, until you came up here."

"It was our last chance, and I'm glad now that I took it. Yes, I'm glad, for it has led to our having it out together now. Vi, I hated coming up here. I swear to you that Archie doesn't care two straws about me, and never has, and never will. He loves you, better to-night than ever before. I swear it, on my soul."

She went forward suddenly, put her arms round Viola, and kissed her.

And then came the tears. Viola's passion of weeping was painful to hear. For some moments these two women cried in each other's arms, like children, and then Peg, with a sort of smile, put Viola into a chair and slipped out of the room.

CHAPTER XXII

ARCHIE obeyed orders again. He entered the bedroom, shut the door, and went over to his wife. He stood up straight. He made no attempt to touch her. He looked very simple and gauche.

" Vi," he said, " I love you, darling."

Viola got up with a cry and flung herself into his arms. She felt herself held strongly. She felt that the two arms round her trembled. She felt Archie's lips upon her face and neck and hair. " That's what I want," she sobbed. " Oh, that's what I have wanted."

Again and again Archie kissed her, and each kiss asked her forgiveness, gave forgiveness, and was eloquent of love. Then he held her away from him.

" Once for all," he said, " tell me."

But she wasn't to be held away, she slipped back into his arms. " I'd grown to think that I didn't matter to you any more," she said brokenly. " You leave me alone so long, always alone. You play your games and work out your hobbies, and I am left at home. I can't come with you, I'm not strong enough. I grant that when you come back you tell me of all that you have done, but any woman would do for that. I am only your housekeeper, that's all. Give me some—a little—of your time. Be with me for a little while each day. Pander to me, feed my vanity, be the lover just a little. I'm a woman and I'm young, and I've got no children.''

She was crying again. He felt her shaking and trembling in his arms. He pressed his kisses on her eyes.

'' I don't ask much,'' she pleaded. '' I married you, but I don't want to be merely the wife, to slip away into being merely the wife. I want to be your sweetheart as well as your wife. I want you to want me. I want *you* as you were when you took me. *I* haven't changed. *I* am the same woman. Why should *you* change and be another man ? I'm not asking you to tie yourself to my dress-strings, to fetch and carry and hold my hand for ever, and be a lap dog. I'm just asking you to remain the man, but to remember that you are *my* man, the man I gave up everything to be with, who won me and owns me and is part of me.''

She put up her arms and fastened them round his neck. All the things that she had kept locked up in her heart until they burned and stung were unloosed.

'' You have given me too much time to think. It's bad to think. I ought to be doing. I ought to have two hours, or an hour, every day, every

little quick day, in which to do something with
you. That would be enough. I should be able
to live on them until the next day. You don't
know what it's been like all this time with you.
No one knows. I can't help having been spoilt
when I was a girl. But I was spoilt, and I came
to you because I loved you better than my life,
and I thought you would spoil me. It's so easy
to spoil me. You've only got to make me think
that I am the one woman you care for. You've
only got to say how sorry you are to go away and
how glad you are to get back, to kiss me and
take an interest in me, and tell me the things you
think I want to hear. Is that so difficult ? "

" No," said Archie.

" Then why haven't you done it—why don't
you do it ? "

" My dear, I—I loved you completely, and I
thought you knew."

" At first I did know ; I couldn't help knowing. It was only when I began to think that I
knew that I wanted to know. And how could *I*
know if you didn't tell me ? I want to be told !
I want to be told ! "

" I wish I were a brighter sort of fellow," said
Hay.

" No, no "—Viola stood on tiptoe and kissed him—" I wouldn't have you different. There isn't a man in the world like you."

" But—but I am far short of all that you want."

" No you're not. You're everything that I want."

" How can that be, Vi ? I don't make you happy."

" You do make me happy, but not completely happy, and that's because you don't think."

Hay drew her closer. He was horribly moved and unmanned and humbled. He would have given a year of his life to be able to say so. He didn't know how to say so. He said, " I will think, Vi ; I will."

Viola pressed her arms more tightly round his neck and put up her tear-stained beautiful face. " It's so easy to make me completely happy, darling," she said. " So easy. Just let me imagine that I'm still engaged to you—not acquired, achieved, taken possession of—but still a woman to win. It isn't difficult to do. A little sudden, unfished-for word does it—that you like my new dress, or the way I've done my hair, or how infinitely you prefer your home

to anyone else's. Those are little things, uncon-
sidered things, but they mean so much to us.
They make all the difference ; they warm and
inspire, and feed and fill. They are not to be
done without, they are absolutely necessary ;
they are the sun and the dew, they freshen and
keep us sweet. There is only one time to say
them, and so say them while you have me, while
I am with you and you are with me. There is
lots of room for silence in the grave."

CHAPTER XXIII

THEY were not aware of the fact that Peg had
tiptoed into the room and had sat down in the
chair by the window, neither did they hear the
little choking sounds that she made as she cried
quietly, all to herself. They stood quite still,
heart to heart, locked in each other's arms, rubbing out, in a sort of way, the creases of unhappiness and doubt, anger, jealousy, and revenge.
They stood quite still, close together, more like
two children who had lost each other and cried
out, running blindly here and there, and had
found each other again. A feeling of great
thankfulness and gratitude pervaded them both.
How bad it might have been, but how good it

was. Viola, with shut eyes, thanked God from the bottom of her heart for this mercy, for His forgiveness. Hay thanked Viola. Both summed themselves up in their particular characteristic manner—Viola with strongly coloured, biting words of abuse, calling herself a demon to have nursed such cruelty in her heart, to have desired so fervently to punish Peg, to have conceived a way so spiteful to rouse Archie's jealousy. She lashed herself with a knotted whip, gave herself no mercy, and finally sent up a prayer that she might outlive these frenzied, tempestuous tempers and become worthy of her husband.

And Hay found himself to be very much wanting. Peg had hinted in the morning at the things which Viola had made plain in the evening. He wished that he had possessed even so much imagination as a plate. Nothing of this would have happened. He never would have imagination, that was certain, but in future— thank God for the future—he would never let himself forget to think. Viola's saying about the grave, the silence of the grave, sent a shudder through his heart. Why, already he had been married how many years? Five? Yes, five years. Viola was a girl of twenty when he had captured her, as she put it. Those years had gone. The rest of them would go as quickly. It was appalling to think that he might only have known how to treat life when waiting to answer to the summons of death. He would make up, if he could, for those five unthinking years. There might not be much time. He was thirty-five—and in the natural order of things Viola would have to spend some years alone. Well, she shouldn't spend them wishing and wishing that he had spoken while there was time. Nor would he, if it pleased Death to leave him alone, spend his waiting years in bitter regrets for the unspoken words.

The past and the future disposed of, there remained the present. The present was good. Hay undid Viola's hands and held her at arm's length and looked at her. He thanked God not that she was beautiful, but that she was young, and that he was thirty-five—only thirty-five. He added thirty to thirty-five, and then he added ten. Forty years would pass all too quickly, but in forty years there was time—he would see to it that there was time.

Peg was obliged to do it, although she knew

that it would break the spell. She blew her nose.
Without attempting to remove his hands from
Viola's shoulders Hay looked round.

" Peg ! " he cried.

" Peg ! " said Viola.

" Yes," came a little voice from behind a
handkerchief—the third that evening—where
the others were she didn't know and didn't care
—" I couldn't help it. Don't be snappy. I
had to come and see."

Viola and Hay bore down upon her together.
" You had a right to come," said Hay.

" It's all through you that you saw—what
you saw," said Viola. She bent down, lifted
Peg up and kissed her.

Hay seized her disengaged hand and pump-
handled it, with a grip that almost would have
given the handle of a racquet a twinge of pain.

" Well," said Peg, " of course we are all very
nice to look at, quite exceptionally nice, although
we've all been through the storm and stress of
the day—is it a day or a week ? it feels like a
week—but if we stand like this any longer we
shall look just a bit foolish. I should like
nothing better than to bellow like a baby, but
I can smell Billy's cigar—he's under the window

—and it won't do for him to find me weeping. He'll think I'm crying about him and begin to buck."

Viola burst out laughing. Hay laughed because she laughed. But both laughs died quickly. They both seemed to be out of the habit, and they both had something to say to Peg, lots to say.

But all that Hay said was "Thanks." And "Thanks" was all that Viola could trust herself to say.

And that was all that Peg wanted, and more.

"And now run away, the pair of you. I'm so happy that if you say another word I shall *have* to make my nose red, and how on earth is a woman with a red nose to give her husband a very bad quarter of an hour?"

CHAPTER XXIV

Bless you, Billy knew all about that bad quarter of an hour. He had already smoked one cigar in order to stave it off, and he was now at the first few pulls of a second. He knew that he must expect it, because hearing nothing of Peg, and not being able to see anything, even from a distance, either of Viola or Archie, he had wandered aimlessly and miserably about the house, trying to conjecture what on earth was up now, and had finally betaken himself to the bedroom landing.

He was surprised to find that Viola's door was wide open. He knocked gently. There was no answer. He entered.

" My Lord ! " he said aloud.

And there was some excuse. He certainly had never seen such a chaotic room. Every conceivable thing that contained a drawer was now wholly devoid of it. Every drawer from every drawable piece of furniture lay empty upon the floor, the bed, and the chairs. Holes gaped where they should have been. Scraps of tissue-paper were scattered everywhere. A box of ordinary bright pins, hastily upset, lay with their small bullet heads pointing this way and that. There were wriggled hairpins among them, and invisible hairpins, and long, straight, dignified, unmistakable hairpins. The fire-place was littered with envelopes and temper-torn letters ; small puffs of cotton-wool sat in surprise where they had fallen. Empty bottles of skin tonics, mostly faced with elaborate labels, elbowed each other upon the mantelboard. Over the post of the bed hung a limp black silk stocking in hopeless loneliness. The room looked just as though it had been ransacked by an invading army of foreign viragoes.

There was a curious streak of tidiness in Billy's composition. Elaborately untidy himself, he disliked very much to see untidiness. It seemed so unnecessary. He gazed about him horror-stricken. The sight of this room almost made him believe that utter ruin had fallen upon every one in the house.

He returned to the landing quickly and stood listening. He was getting awfully sick of loneliness. Where were they all? What were they all doing? Where the dickens was Viola? He would rather undergo another rush and tear scene with her than be obliged to meander about without a soul to speak to. There wasn't even a cat up with whom to pass the time of night. Night? By Jove, it would be day soon. It was twenty minutes to twelve. Good Lord, what a day!

It was absolutely unbearable. Amazingly sick of himself, utterly out of taste with himself, he never in his life wanted so keenly to find someone else with an equally big grievance. He looked into his dressing-room and barked his shins against his trouser-case. Obviously Meakin had finished packing and gone to bed. Had he gone to bed? Meakin would be better than no one. He had known him for—well, it didn't matter how long. He simply hated to feel that he was drifting into that objectionable time of life when he was able to say, " Let me see, yes, it must be seven, eight—by Jove, it's twelve years ago."

" Oh, dash everything ! "

He went downstairs, walked listlessly about the hall, gazed distastefully at his empty glass, and his cigar ash, and the low-burnt candles that had guttered in a blasé sort of way, and turned into the passage that led to the kitchen.

There was a light under the door still. He would go in. He must hear himself speak. He hesitated and then opened the door. He saw Meakin lying back in his deck-chair. The lamp was burning steadily on the corner of the table, and the open window framed a small square of star-mottled sky. But Meakin's head had fallen back on a cushion, and his book lay face down upon his knees. One arm had slipped down and its limp fingers trailed on the linoleum. With wide-open mouth the man, the artist, the consummate workman was enjoying a beautiful sleep.

" Well I'm blessed ! " thought Billy. " Sleep-in' ! at such a moment ! "

He took a coin out of his pocket and rapped the table with it.

Meakin stirred.

Billy persisted. If Meakin had been a friend he would have flung something at him. He disliked familiarity, however.

Meakin shut his mouth and swallowed, and licked his lips, and breathed heavily.

" Meakin," said Billy sharply, " Meakin."

" All right," said Meakin, " let it pass. Chuck away a certain tenner, and then don't blame me because you didn't have your shirt on the best thing in racing."

" Meakin ! " The rather stupid name rang through the room.

The owner of it opened his eyes with an effort, shut them again, reopened them, turned and regarded the interrupter vaguely, annoyedly, interestedly, respectfully. Meakin rose.

" I am required, Sir William ? " he asked, gravely straightening his back hair.

Billy found himself at a loss. Meakin was not required. It was rather awkward. He would manufacture a grievance.

" Now look here, Meakin," he said in an almost parental way, " the last thing in the world that I want to do is to er—interfere with your private life, and that sort of thing."

" Exactly, Sir William," replied the man, with a dangerous glint in his eyes.

" Well "—Billy had caught the glint—" I say I don't. I haven't up to now."

" No indeed, Sir William."

" Well, then. . . . What I came along on purpose to say is this. If you make a practice of sittin' up late night after night like this, how can you expect to look fit ? Do you see ? "

Meakin studied his master's face analytically. What was his game ? What in the name of all that was wonderful had he come into the kitchen for ? Why had he chosen a time when he was naturally upset to make sudden tender inquiries as to the health of a servant ? Was it possible that he had dallied a little too familiarly with the whisky ?

" I'm sure it's very kind of you to trouble, Sir William," replied Meakin cautiously.

Billy glanced uneasily at the clock. That bad quarter of an hour was relentlessly coming nearer and nearer. Hang it all, he would face it boldly. He wasn't afraid of Peg. He wasn't afraid of anything that she might say or do. She was not one of the best. She was the very best. What he was afraid of was that he had made an egregious fool of himself and would be obliged to own to it. He never had owned to such a thing before. That is to say, he never had been obliged to own to such a thing before. Yes, he would face it.

He turned to the door. "That's all, Meakin," he said, "I thought I would give you a hint. Good-night."

"Good-night, Sir William. Permit me to thank you kindly."

"Oh, not a bit."

Billy looked into the dark passage and drew up short. After all, there was no great hurry —and he didn't know where Peg was or if she wanted to be bothered just yet.

"Nice room, this," he said, "eh?"

"Very nice indeed, Sir William."

"Airy, and fresh, and so on. What?"

"Very indeed, Sir William."

"And I've never noticed that before," said Billy. He went over to the window on the left of the fire-place. "Opens outwards, by Jove!

Ah, very sensible, and rather tweeky. Oh, very nice, very nice."

Meakin smiled faintly. It was not whisky. But his speculations had not brought him to any definite conclusion.

He did not think that he was called upon to make any reply.

Billy turned towards the door again. He began to feel in a kindlier humour with himself. Not many men would take the trouble to look after the health of their servants and the hygiene of their servants' quarters. But again the darkness of the passage gave him an uncomfortable jar. The passage led to the hall, and once in the hall . . . well, Peg might hear him and either come down or call.

" What's your book ? " he asked. He picked it up and examined it interestedly. " Oh, you go in for improvin' readin', I see. That's right. Always a good thing to read well if you can be bothered to read. Her ladyship lent you this, I take it ? "

" No, Sir William. I subscribe to Mudie's."

" The devil you do ! "

He put the book down. Not being a reading man himself he felt a sort of admiration for

Meakin. He considered that a man who could actually sit down and read that sort of stuff must have something in him. His kindlier humour broadened. None of the men in his set could boast of a man like Meakin. It only showed what a fine thing good influence was on the lower class. Subscribed to Mudie's too. Yes, there was no doubt about it. Meakin owed him a good deal. He was very glad.

Now he would go. Why be nervous about seeing Peg? He couldn't see any real reason for saying that he was sorry. Much better let sleeping dogs lie. She knew as well as he did that he did not intend to go to London with Viola in the morning. He had packed his things merely in order to be in the room with Peg for a bit. That was all. She knew that all right. Oh, bless you, she always knew. All the same he . . . well, now that he happened to be in the kitchen, it seemed rather unkind not to unbend somewhat to the man who had served him well for many years. He would take it very kindly, and sympathy never was thrown away.

" Find the place a bit dull, eh ? " he asked, without looking at Meakin.

" Well, Sir William, I do. If I may say so, it does seem a pity to evade the London season."

Billy's eyes fell on a box of cigars. " How do you like 'em ? "

Meakin could tell from the tone of the question that Sir William believed that he had caught him out. He was amused.

" I haven't smoked any others for years, sir," he replied.

Billy became rather wide-eyed. Here was frankness if you like.

Meakin continued. " On an average, I smoke four of those a day, Sir William, all the year round."

" Well, of all the . . ."

" I have dealt with Lewis since I paid my father's account. I have a thousand at a time. You will remember that I recommended the brand to you, sir ? "

" Oh, I'm sorry," said Billy ; " I mean—yes, so you did." He turned away rather hastily. Quite an exceptional person, Meakin. There was no doubt. But that was a rather unpleasant way of his, that way of taking advantage of a mistake. However, there it was.

Meakin remained expressionless. Inwardly he was enjoying the biggest laugh that he had had that day. He was now very well aware of the fact that Sir William was killing time with him. He wondered how long he would remain. He saw his master's frequent glances towards the door. He had noticed that every time he had got to the door, he jibbed suddenly. Not for the first time this well-groomed, good-looking man, just slightly running to plumpness here and there, reminded Meakin of a very bright, middle-aged, pet dog, who, although knowing perfectly well that he was being whistled for, hung back because he could see in his mind's eye the whip behind the whistler's back.

" Any idea of being married yet, Meakin ? " asked Billy pleasantly.

" No woman will receive me permanently, Sir William, until I lose all interest in my work."

" I see. Well, perhaps you're right. A great lottery, marriage, until you have acquired an absolute knowledge of women."

Again Billy's eyes were fixed on the door.

" Nice thing, a dresser, I always think. Remind me to collect a few really corkin' plates, and look out for a genuine Jacobean thing, will you ? Go well in my room at Beauly."

" I will, Sir William."

Meakin closed his book, shut the cigar box, and only half hid a yawn behind his hand.

Billy noticed these obvious preparations. Again his unwilling eye fell on the door. What dashed nonsense! He *wanted* to tell Peg that he was sorry for having made a fool of himself. Confession was good for the soul. " Well, good-night."

Before Meakin could reply he was alone, and then he laughed softly, picked up the book, the box, and the lamp, and went up to bed.

Billy went boldly through the hall and out into the passage that led to the staircase. Under the staircase there was a door which opened on to the pathway round the house. Billy chose the door. Round and round the house he prowled, smoking without enjoyment, blind to the exquisite beauty of the night. All his senses were concentrated into one—hearing. He listened eagerly to every sound. He heard the rumble of voices in Peg's bedroom and watched the un-blinking light. Then he saw two shadows, and then a third, and heard the sound—the unaccus-tomed sound—of laughing. Voices came again —a deep one, a silver one, and one that was like a bell. Then there was silence. A door was shut. After a moment another was shut, and there was a moving light in Viola's room.

Then, watching intently, he saw a cautious hand draw back the curtain from Peg's window, saw a beautiful head appear and disappear. Then he heard the sound of singing—soft, delicious singing.

" That's Peg," he thought. " My Lord, the others have made it up."

He pitched his cigar away, put his hand up to his tie, pulled down his waistcoat, re-entered the house, very deliberately shut and bolted the door, blew out the lamp in the hall, and went upstairs. And as he went he whistled.

CHAPTER XXV

PEG heard someone moving about in the dressing-room. She smiled, went quickly to the dressing-table, sat down in front of the glass, and made a collection of all the pins that were in her hair. When the brown flood had fallen over her shoulders, she began to use a brush vigorously.

Billy opened the door.

" Hallo ! " he said.

" My dear Billy," cried Peg, " how you made me jump."

" Sorry ! "

Billy had become gloomy. He knew from every sign that all unhappy things had come to an end. Peg herself never had looked more cheery nor more delicious. Nothing had been said to him by any of them—Peg, Viola, or Archie. He felt himself to be, therefore, the only one with the right to be unhappy. He took up a martyred position, with both elbows on the chest of drawers. He heaved a deep sigh.

" Have you ever seen such a lovely moonlight night ? " asked Peg.

There was a pause.

" I don't think," said Billy slowly, " that I shall ever be the same man again."

" Perhaps that's rather a good thing."

Billy stretched out a hand and commenced to open and shut the doors of a large red leather dressing-bottle case. The noise was small but irritating. He pushed the thing away.

" I knew all along that you and Archie were play-actin'."

" Oh yes, of course," said Peg.

That was all right. Then there would be no need after all for a humble confession.

" I'm not a dashed fool, y' know," he continued quickly. " What ? Archie's one of the best, but, hang it, not quite the kind of chap you'd fancy in that sort of way, eh ? "

Peg made no reply. The brush went busily.

" All the same, I saw another perfectly white hair just now."

" Really ? " Peg was greatly interested. " Did you catch it or did it get away ? "

" Oh, rot," grumbled Billy. He wandered nearer. He went to the window and flicked the curtains. He picked up a hairpin and twisted it into whimsical shapes.

" Anyway," he said, " I've made it all right between those two."

Peg's hair hung conveniently over her smiling face. " Yes, so I see. Very nice of you."

Billy caught up the long hanging sleeve of the kimono, and rumpled it. The word Peg applied to his expression was one that would have rankled in his mind for weeks—sheepish.

" I say, Peggy dear, I want to tell you something ; you won't chip me if I do ? "

" My dear William, I do paint sometimes, but I'm no sculptor."

He went down on his knees suddenly, and threw his arms round her and put his face on her shoulder.

" Peggy, I'm dashed sorry, most awfully dashed sorry about all this. I did it because—because I've always flirted; you've never minded, why should you? And I thought I had lost—what the devil shall I say?—my—well then, attraction, and I just wanted to see. Do you understand? You're the only woman I love, or ever could love. You're not a woman—you're *the* woman, do you see what I mean? You little witch, I don't love you, I adore you. I always have and I always shall. Don't you know that, darlin' old gel? "

Peg put her hand under his chin, tilted up his boyish face and kissed it.

" Yes, dear old man," she said, " of course I do. But you'll never do it again . . . will you? "

And then she put her arms round his shoulders and his head on her bosom, as though he were her child. In a sort of way he was.

THE END

Printed at The Chapel River Press, Kingston, Surrey.